THE HUNDRED
WELLS OF SALAGA

EAST ATLANTA

THE HUNDRED WELLS OF SALAGA

Ayesha Harruna Attah

Other Press

New York

First published in Nigeria by Cassava Republic Press in 2018

Production editor: Yvonne E. Cárdenas
Book design: Allan Castillo Rivas

10 9 8 7 6 5 4 3 2 1

LIBRARY OF CONGRESS CATALOGING-IN-PUBLICATION DATA

Names: Attah, Ayesha Harruna.
Title: The hundred wells of Salaga / Ayesha Harruna Attah.
Description: New York : Other Press, [2019]
Identifiers: LCCN 2018023011 (print) | LCCN 2018025554 (ebook) |
    ISBN 9781590519967 (ebook) | ISBN 9781590519950 (paperback)
Subjects: LCSH: Ghana—History—To 1957—Fiction. | Slavery—Ghana—
    History—19th century—Fiction. | Slave trade—Ghana—History—
    19th century—Fiction. | BISAC: FICTION / Contemporary Women. |
    FICTION / Coming of Age. | FICTION / Cultural Heritage. |
    GSAFD: Historical fiction.
Classification: LCC PR9379.9.H37 (ebook) | LCC PR9379.9.H37 H86 2019 (print)
    | DDC 823/.92—dc23
LC record available at https://lccn.loc.gov/2018023011

*The clan that is great in number
is also great in strength*

—Gurma proverb

AMINAH'S FAMILY

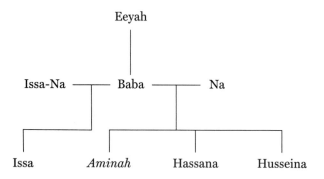

Eeyah

Issa-Na —— Baba —— Na

Issa   *Aminah*   Hassana   Husseina

OTHERS

Wofa Sarpong —*farmer; buys Aminah*

Sahada — *pawned off by her father*

Maigida — *landlord*

Khadija — *kidnapped by Moro*

WURCHE'S FAMILY

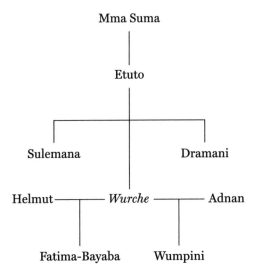

Mma Suma

Etuto

Sulemana   Dramani

Helmut —— *Wurche* —— Adnan

Fatima-Bayaba   Wumpini

OTHERS

Jaji —*Wurche's teacher*

Shaibu — *Prince of Salaga-Kpembe*

Baki — *Wurche's horse*

Moro — *slave raider*

Fatima — *Wurche's childhood friend*

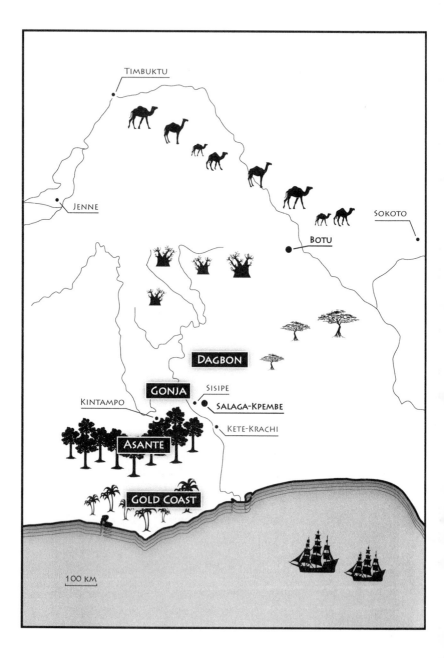

Aminah

The caravans could come at dawn. The caravans could come when the sun was highest in the sky. The caravans could come when midnight had cloaked everything in velvety blue. The only sure thing was that the Sokoto caravans would come well before the end of the dry season. But now, that had changed. For weeks, Aminah and the rest of Botu were not even sure the caravans would come at all. Even though rain clouds had not yet emptied, lightning lit up the sky in the distance and thunder boomed. The grass had already started to grow tall. And there was talk of horsemen getting closer. Horsemen who razed everything to the ground. Horsemen who scared off the caravansary. Horsemen who stole people. It wasn't a good sign. Aminah's father needed to go to Jenne to sell his shoes. Aminah's family needed to sell their food.

A week before the rains started, Aminah heard the thumping of drums just as she was about to prepare the evening meal. She dropped the onions in her hands, thanked Otienu that misfortune had been averted, and hurriedly made for her twin sisters in her mother's hut. The girls rushed to join a throng of their village sisters and brothers belting out songs of welcome. She could barely hear their own songs, drowned out as they were by the caravan's drums. Aminah and the twins squeezed themselves through tiny gaps to move closer to the front.

Camels and their riders filed by, moving almost in tandem with the beat of the drums, followed by women balancing enormous cloud-shaped bundles on their heads. They were trailed by donkeys saddled with sky-high loads, then porters, pitiful-looking men and women burdened with baskets and pans, wearing nothing but strips of cloth covering their private parts. Hassana, the elder twin, flapped her arm excitedly at a figure in the distance that appeared to float above everyone else in the procession. The madugu! Aminah's heart twitched with excitement. The madugu, a majestic figure riding a gigantic horse, lifted his hand to salute the crowd. It was as if he moved and the ground shook. It was what he wore. It was his horse, his dance, the fact that he'd seen places in the world none of them had. It was his power. He was the highlight of the caravans. At the end of the procession, boys in rags, banging on calabashes, collected money from those who would give it to them. They left her feeling sad. On seeing the beggars, the crowd moved forward to stay in line with the madugu, as if just by looking at him, his majesty would rub off on them. The air was thick with the smell of caged rain, an herby livestock odor, spices, soups boiling. As a pink evening light began to stroke the sky, the excitement of the crowd mounted.

"Make way for the head of Botu, make way for Obado," said a voice that could only belong to Eeyah, Aminah's grandmother.

Eeyah and her group of griottes had surrounded Obado, so he was hard to see. Aminah pictured his smock billowing about his torso, his hat askance, his expression serious, his short arms swinging with self-importance. When Obado emerged, he was wearing a smock but no hat. He set himself a few paces ahead of everyone, the large leather pouch slung across the paunch of his small body announcing that he was there to collect money.

The madugu rode his horse towards Obado to begin negotiations on the caravan toll. The toll exacted from the Sokoto caravan was more than all the other caravans combined. It was also the most difficult to negotiate. Once, the caravan stayed in Botu for more than a week because the madugu and Obado couldn't come to an agreement.

The madugu—his robes a rich blend of blue and violet, his head turbaned in white, his dark skin glistening—swayed left and right with each drumbeat, and his balled fist appeared to grind the air above his head each time his horse strode forward. Aminah wondered what it was like to wield such power. It made him comfortable in his body in a way Obado was not. But it made sense: he was in charge of thousands of travelers. Botu held only a few hundred people.

When the madugu jumped off his horse and stood before Obado, Botu's father—the man people went to, to keep the peace—looked like a mere child. The drumming thrummed to a climax and then dwindled.

The two men embraced and the madugu bent over to speak to Obado, while signaling for his men to get the caravan settled in the zongo. Together they made for Obado's house, trailed by Eeyah and her griottes, whose high-pitched voices sang the madugu and Obado's praises.

Aminah dragged the twins home. Na would be annoyed that the girls hadn't already cooked and started selling to the caravans.

Aminah watched a glob of shea butter liquefy into a golden yellow oil, her mind on the caravan. She thought of the madugu. Eeyah once told her that he had twenty wives and was still searching. When she'd told her friends, they started conspiring to set themselves in his path. To be a twenty-first wife. What was admirable about that? Aminah preferred the idea of traveling on a camel or horse with a sack full of shoes, doing the kind of work Baba did. Making something with one's hands and then traveling far to sell it. The oil bubbled and spurted and cast its nuttiness into the air. Aminah rested her head on her palm and stared at the oil. No woman in Botu made shoes. They all worked the land. She needed to talk to Baba. What if she made shoes?

A knock hit the back of her head, giving her a slight shock. It had to be Na, who couldn't stand Aminah's daydreaming. Or Eeyah, who took pleasure in startling her. Aminah turned and met Issa-Na's cold gaze. The woman's eyes were piercingly white, her hair plaited with thread and styled cone-like above her head. Prickly. Images of porcupines seeped into Aminah's mind whenever Issa-Na appeared. There was a woman in second place and bitter about it. She was all the proof Aminah needed that being a twenty-first wife was not desirable.

Aminah looked at her stepmother who was mother to Issa, her only brother. She arranged her face to look as respectful as possible.

"You're going to burn the maasa," said Issa-Na. "There's nothing worse than burned maasa."

The woman was right. The shea oil was boiling in black bubbles at the edges of the pot. Aminah took the pot off the fire. Issa-Na turned on her heel and left the kitchen before Aminah could thank her for her counsel.

Aminah returned the pot to the fire, scooped out balls of the rice and millet paste and lowered them into the oil, excitement building in her chest. The maasa turned golden brown. One never knew what the caravans brought. Into a big brass basin, she piled a large pot of millet porridge, honey, sour cow's milk and several calabash half spheres cupped together. She put the maasa on a smaller tray, then carried her basin outside, where Na, slightly obscured by the steam rising from a large pot, churned her tuo. Na's tuo was popular because it was fluffy. The family secret was to sprinkle rice flour into the millet paste.

Na called her over. "Did I see that woman hit you?"

Aminah nodded slowly. The knock had only startled her; it wasn't that painful. And as mean as Issa-Na was to her, she didn't want her to get into trouble. "The oil was burning."

"Next time don't give her a reason to touch you," said Na.

Na said that because Issa-Na's skin was lighter than theirs, she generally got her way. Na said a long time ago something had poisoned people into thinking the lighter you were, the better you were. She said Issa-Na looked uncooked, that in a perfect world, Aminah would be considered more beautiful than Issa-Na. Then Na said, "But you can't eat beauty."

She stared at Issa-Na's hut, then returned her gaze to Aminah. "Why are you still here? The caravan people are hungry. Fast, fast!"

Aminah dragged the twins out of the compound. The girls greeted old ladies who thought themselves too old to take part in the activities but didn't want to miss out on any gossip, so set up their stools close to the zongo.

In the evening light, the tents of the zongo were already standing tall and comfortable, as if they'd always belonged on Aminah's people's lands. Others were still taking shape as men of the caravan and men from Botu sliced at patches of tall grass. People carried sand from the water hole and used it to shape blocks; some women were snapping off branches while others braided grass to form walls. The zongo had turned into a fair. Fires crackled, drums beat. The air smelled of smoke, meat and alcohol. Aminah wanted to do Na proud by selling off all they'd brought, but when she arrived, every available sitting place was filled with sellers. They had no choice but to walk around peddling their food. Aminah distributed it, handing Hassana the maasa, and the younger twin, Husseina, the sour milk. She carried the porridge.

"Maasakokodanono," sang the twins who had inherited Eeyah's musical tongue. "Maasakokodanono."

Narrow paths separated clumps of tents. The ground was littered with animal bones, shreds of cloth, morsels of half-eaten meals, broken pots, tufts of hair, puddles of liquid. Outside one tent, a woman recognized Aminah and said she'd been looking forward to eating her maasa since her last trip from Kano. She spoke in Hausa, the language of the caravans, not Gurma, the language of Botu. Aminah wondered about Kano. If it was small, like Botu. Or if it was the way Baba described Jenne: a town of clay-coated houses with paths in which one could get lost. A town that hugged two arms of a river. A town with a mosque that reached the skies, large enough to hold thousands of worshippers. Her mind went to other places Baba had visited to sell his shoes: Timbuktu, Salaga. He hadn't been to Kano.

The woman sighed, snapping Aminah out of her daze. The twins were already wandering off, so she thanked the woman, gathered Hassana and Husseina, and continued weaving around the zongo. Some travelers were selling goods, while others had gone straight to sleep, dirty feet splayed on their mats. At one tent, hundreds of glimmering lights caught Aminah's attention. It was a stall with mirrors of various sizes, some as tall as she was, others small, just large enough to see one's face. It wasn't every day she caught her reflection, and the owner was nowhere in sight, so she set her porridge down and took a quick look in a small silver mirror with an ivory handle carved with flowered vines. On its frame were two fearful-looking lizard-like animals with egg-shaped eyes, scaly bodies, and multiple limbs twisting around each other. She gave in to the lure of the glass. The only times she saw her face were before events in the village. Only Obado's wife owned a mirror. Every villager would troop outside their hut, fix their hair and face, then move on to the ceremony. Aminah observed her thick eyebrows, the hairs flying in all directions. Her nose was small and expanded slightly when she flared her nostrils. She was about to stick out her tongue, when, through the mirror, she locked eyes with someone behind her. She almost screamed, feeling like her insides were about to leave her body, but her mother had told her never to show fear in public. She turned and faced an old man with hair the color of heavy rain clouds.

"I see you like my mirrors," he said, and in his eyes Aminah recognized her father—a kind man who worked and never stopped.

"Sorry ..."

"In some places," he said, "they say if you look too long into a mirror, it will steal your soul. In other places, they say you become vain if you stare at yourself too long. Who is right?"

Aminah checked behind her to make sure he wasn't talking to someone else. Someone used to riddles, maybe.

"What do you think?"

Suddenly, she remembered the twins. She'd forgotten they were with her.

"I'm sorry." She bent to pick up her pot of porridge. If she didn't find her sisters, what words would she use to tell her parents?

She wound around the zongo three times before coming upon a group of turbaned men sitting around a fire, laughing as if they had no worries. Next to them, the twins sat on a raffia mat before a pile of wooden dolls wrapped with a rainbow of beads and cowries. As she made her way to them, one of the turbaned men stopped talking, fixed his gaze on her, then flung his ringed hand in the air to beckon her. The hairs on her forearms stood up, and she stole a glance at the twins, who were entranced by the dolls. Aminah was certain she could quickly sell to the man and collect her sisters. She was there to sell food, she reasoned, and here was a potential customer. She walked over.

"What are you selling, Beauty?" asked the man. He smiled, and his teeth shone bright white. His eyes, shaded by his turquoise turban, stayed trained on her. He seemed to wear a permanent smirk.

"Maasa, sour milk and millet porridge."

"*My* mother makes the best millet porridge. Let's see how yours compares."

Aminah set down her pot, but her hand shook so much that the man grabbed her wrist to steady her, and firmly but gently lowered her body to his level.

"Relax," he whispered. Then shouted: "Who wants to try Beauty's porridge?"

The men all wanted it. She started serving the one who had waved her over, but he pointed to the others, indicating that she serve his friends first and save him for last. The bonfire heated up everything in her body, speeding up the beat of her heart, oozing beads of sweat from her skin and leaving her heady. She looked over at the twins, still playing with the dolls, and in doing so, spilled porridge on one man's white robe. As she stared, terrified, at the mess, he mopped at it with another part of his robe and waved her away. She served everyone, took their cowries, and returned to the man in the turquoise turban. As she poured out his bowl of porridge into a calabash, she felt his gaze on her. She handed it to him.

"Sit with me, Beauty."

He had provided her with quite a few customers and she needed to get her bowls back, so she relented. She sat down and tried not to let the fear in her chest show on her face. She checked on the twins. They hadn't even noticed her. The man wrapped his wiry arm around Aminah's waist and tugged her closer. He looked small, but his pull was strong. He slurped his porridge. His friends ate and chatted.

"I disagree. Babatu's men are indiscriminate," bellowed one. "There are people who become slaves, and there are people who should be left alone. Those men go for anyone. No one—highborn or low—is safe from their raids. And they are giving people who ride horses a bad name."

"Relax, Mus," said the man who'd called Aminah over, laughing. None of his teeth hid. "Babatu and his men need us. If he and his slave raiders start attacking traders, where will they get their supplies? We are their link to the Europeans and their goods. Also, how many people are buying their slaves now that the Europeans say they have outlawed slavery?"

"He's right," said another. "Although, there are still quite a few Europeans who ask for slaves."

"Most of my porters were captured by Babatu's soldiers," said a third man.

The man beside Aminah curved his index finger, encircled with a knobbed silver ring, and spooned up a globule of porridge left in the calabash. She waited for his verdict, hoping it would free her.

"What's your name?" he said.

"Aminah."

"Beautiful Queen Aminah," he beamed. That did not reassure her.

"Did you like the porridge?" she asked.

He put his hand on her thigh and the pads of his fingers settled on her the way one's feet steady themselves on new ground: on tiptoes at first, and then with all of one's weight. His thumb and forefingers pinched the cloth covering the flesh on her thighs and then he found the opening of her wrapper and his thumb made contact with her skin. He traced circles and warmth grew in that area, threatening to climb up, but she willed the heat to stay under his fingers. She didn't understand why her body was enjoying what he was doing, although it didn't feel right. His fingers drew lines higher and higher up her thighs. His friends still talked, oblivious or pretending to be. She focused on her cover cloth puckering up and down every time he moved his hand. He drew his face closer to hers. His hot breath was inches away.

"I'll tell you about the porridge if we can go somewhere," he whispered.

His hand slithered up her thigh and his fingers were about to touch her triangle when she leapt up. She grabbed his bowl and hurried to gather those that had been left on the ground.

"Hassana, Husseina," she shouted, running to them. "Home!"

She could barely steady her shaking hands as she made towards the twins.

"Beautiful Aminah," the man drawled and leaned back, staring at her.

"Can we stay a little longer?" whined Hassana.

Aminah ignored her. She wanted to be shrouded under something heavy. As she made her way out of the zongo, the grass beeped and bubbled and chirped and croaked and whistled and rustled and danced and bent. Overcome by fear of the world it concealed—leopards, jackals, crocodiles, horsemen, turbaned men—she made the twins run all the way home.

She herded them into Na's hut and left the pots and calabashes unwashed. Na would talk and talk the next day about the mess, about the leftover food attracting rats and the rats bringing snakes, but after the experience of that evening, Na's words would be a soothing balm. As she made for the hut she shared with Eeyah, she heard the clang of metal hitting the ground. Baba. He always dropped things. She went to him.

A small fire lit the room, held by the beautiful lamp with the fan-shaped crown and intertwined metal staff the blacksmith had gifted to Baba.

"What do you think?" He lifted a tall brown boot embroidered with red thread. It wasn't his best embroidery, but Aminah always felt warm inside when he asked for her opinion, and the boot *was* intriguing.

"Beautiful." She settled on the lone stool in the room. "Baba, I'm scared," she said, after a beat of silence.

"Why?"

She couldn't tell him about the turbaned man—she couldn't tell anyone. Still, the conversation about Babatu and his raiding horsemen provided her with fodder.

"The horsemen. What if they come while you're away?"

Baba was quiet. It was a measured, calm quiet. Not the oppressive, heavy breathing of someone who didn't like silence. His quietness was his essence, and it had a way of cushioning the rough edges of the room. Baba had spread a gray sheet on the floor, where he piled his shoes. He reached for a knife, snipped a loose thread off the boot, and added it to the pile.

"Nowhere is safe," he said, after a while. "But we can't live in fear. People keep talking of horsemen as if it's a new thing. If it's not the horsemen, it'll be some disease, or a drought. There'll always be an unknown thing coming for us. As for the horsemen, it's because of places that have kings and queens. It's in places like Botu, where everyone is equal, that you don't find slaves. But there aren't many Botus left. All we can do is pray for Otienu's continued protection. Take care of your mothers for me. You are in charge now till I come back. Just don't dream too much."

His large eyelids drooped, shaded by the light from the lamp. It was as if Otienu had shaped every part of his being in a gentle mold.

Three days later, he left as a furor of drums announced the caravans' departure at the break of dawn. Aminah and the twins saw him off, their scrawny arms flapping up and down to wave him goodbye, but Baba and his albino donkey were swallowed by the crowd. They would resume life as usual, Aminah thought, until he returned in a few months.

Wurche

To prevent the bustle of Salaga from encroaching on them, the royalty of the twin towns of Salaga-Kpembe restricted Kpembe to royals. Everybody else was welcome to stay in Salaga. But to Wurche, Salaga was like the soups her grandmother often cooked, bubbling with meat and fish of all types. It was home to Mossis, Yorubas, Hausas, Dioulas, Dagombas. While visiting, she often gazed with longing at the European weapons that had come up from the coast, at the horses brought down by the Mossis, and listened to the banter between the traders who wanted to get rid of their wares and the buyers who simply liked to bargain. Everything was for sale in Salaga. Etuto, her father, often took her to the Friday races here, but earlier in the week he had taken her brothers to meet the other chiefs of Kpembe at an emergency gathering in Kete-Krachi, a town with a powerful oracle who had become a mediator for kingdoms in the area. Wurche and her grandmother, Mma Suma, were therefore representing the family in the men's absence. The women headed for the racecourse, passing by shea trees, their branches spotted with the oval bodies of a thousand storks. The women continued past broken-down huts and uncountable wells.

"Coins from every corner of the world!"

"Embroidered leather shoes!"

"Maasa maasa maasa!"

At the entrance to the racecourse, a madman danced as men thrummed on wide-rimmed drums—*padada padada padada*. Matted hair. Dust coating his body. *Pa pa pa padada pa pa.* He gripped a large piece of meat. He jigged his shoulders, slowly lifting one knee, then the other. *Pa pa pa.* Every muscle fiber of his brown arms and legs moved. The drummers pounced on the skins of their drums. *Pa pa pa padadadada.* Manic fire lit his eyes. He swayed left, then right. Wurche thought he would fall.

The racecourse was haloed in dust as horses and their riders sped by. While coming to Salaga was a treat, Wurche could do without the actual race because Shaibu always won. The old Kpembewura's son was in the lead, his gray horse caparisoned with a blue velvet saddlecloth and a matching hood. She flung out her hand, willing the other riders to go faster.

Mma pinched the underside of Wurche's arm. "These are the things that stop you from getting a husband."

The old ladies of Kpembe said Wurche should have been born a boy, that all she lacked was a lump dangling between her legs. They said she had pebbles for breasts and a platter for buttocks. Etuto said Wurche's slender body made her a natural racer, but he never let her take part in the Friday races. It just isn't done, he said. The old women of Kpembe also said she was her father's favorite, but she didn't agree with that. He was selective with the things he let her do.

"Smile," said Mma. "Frowning doesn't suit a round face."

"This is a waste of my time. I should also be in Kete-Krachi."

"Your father said it was not right for a girl to go with them. And he's right. The oracle of Dente is not to be joked with. He once led the Asante to victory by causing heavy rainfall. If you're not Allah and you can make it rain, aren't you to be feared? Besides, this trouble between the chiefs could turn ugly when the Kpembewura dies. I was a little girl when the last war broke out because the three lines couldn't decide on a successor. Believe me, these things happen in cycles."

Wurche barely heard her grandmother. If Dramani of all people had gone to Kete-Krachi, she should, too. Anything her brother did, Wurche felt she should be given the chance to try. Mma once told her that Wurche's body was filled with a man's spirit and Dramani's, a woman's spirit. Mma said it had to be Wurche's mother's parting gift to Etuto, since she had died giving birth to *his* child, and hadn't always been treated well.

Wurche observed her grandmother, who wasn't watching the races either. The old woman was certainly scouting for potential grandsons-in-law. Wurche scoured the crowd: dignitaries from Dagbon in flamboyant indigo-striped smocks shaped like lunga drums; the Salaga landlords who loved to skimp on the taxes they owed Etuto and the other Kpembe chiefs; Hausa traders with white turbans encircling their heads; Mossi men in their long billowing smocks holding on to their donkeys; a sprinkling of white men; Dom Francisco de Sousa, the Brazilian who occasionally came up from the coast to buy goods. Originally from Sokoto, Dom Sousa was sold as a slave and ended up in a land called Bahia until he bought his freedom and returned to the Gold Coast. It was said that he liked coming up to Salaga during the races because it reminded him of Sokoto. There were women selling maasa and sour milk; men carrying smocks for sale; slaves fetching wood for their masters, their necks ringed with brass. The smell of rot wafted over. It was the one thing she didn't like about Salaga: waste everywhere, with vultures left to do the work of cleaning up.

Commotion from the crowd returned Wurche's attention to the racetrack. Somebody had overtaken Shaibu. She leaned forward. The games were finally getting interesting. The new rider shot by on a white horse decorated with a leopard-skin saddlecloth.

"That man is either very courageous or a fool," said Wurche. "But that someone is letting Shaibu know he's not talented pleases me greatly."

The brave rider gained a considerable lead. The others lagged behind, not daring to close in on Shaibu. When the white horse crossed the finish line, the crowd erupted. Wurche shrieked. The rider dismounted and waited for the prince and the others to get to the finish line.

A small throng gathered before Shaibu and seemed to bow and scrape to his every word. Shaibu took the winner's wrist and lifted it high. The crowd roared in applause again. Shaibu nodded at the victor and didn't seem sour.

"Who is that man who's managed to get his way with Shaibu?" asked Wurche.

"Moro," said Mma. "I heard Etuto say he brought in what must have been hundreds of slaves into Salaga, just the other day. With time, his reputation could reach the likes of Babatu and Samory Toure."

"I haven't heard of him."

"You don't know everything, Wurche, especially when it comes to business in Salaga. To you, it's insignificant, isn't it? But people like Moro keep Salaga alive. You even grew up with him."

When Wurche was a child, explained Mma, Moro lived in Kpembe. He was Shaibu's tail, always wearing a dirty sack. Wurche ransacked her brain. She couldn't remember him.

They made for the front to congratulate the winner as was customary. This was the first time in a long while that the winner wasn't Shaibu, and Wurche was itching to meet Moro. They stood quietly, waiting for Shaibu to acknowledge them. Wurche had to bite her tongue; she wanted to be done with Shaibu as quickly as possible.

Men came and went, shaking hands with Shaibu and Moro. When Shaibu noticed Mma and Wurche, he said, "Good afternoon, Mma Suma. Good afternoon, wild princess of Kpembe, the breaker of my heart."

"How is your mother's family?" said Mma, bending her left knee, grimacing in pain. Wurche glowered. The woman had been complaining about aches in her knees for the past month. Shaibu was the one who should defer to her, not the other way around. But because he was a man, because he was a prince, Mma couldn't help it.

"In good health," said Shaibu.

"Your father's family?"

"In good health."

"How are you yourself?"

"In good health."

"We thank Allah." Mma turned to Moro. "This was a fine, fine race. And congratulations to you."

Shaibu, Mma and Moro turned to regard Wurche, who had forgotten that she too had to extend her congratulations. Something in Moro's face, in his manner, shook her confidence.

"My granddaughter seems to have forgotten her manners," said Mma.

"Well done," said Wurche.

Just then, a loud, throaty cry punctured the excited chatter. It was the kind of scream that raised hairs on the backs of necks.

Everyone looked about, confused. A woman emerged, barely clothed, heavy metal ringed around her neck, and charged towards them. Moro ended her rampage, suddenly appearing behind her and whacking her on the shoulder. As her body crumpled, he bent over and helped her sit up, then lifted her off the ground and slung her over his shoulder. The woman, her brown skin blushed with red soil, writhed in pain; from her throat came a low rumbling. Who was this man? He cooed at her like a father admonishing a difficult child and patted her back. A man approached from the direction the woman had come, a chain in his hand, and looked about. Moro went to him.

"One of the wild ones," explained Shaibu. Then added, clearly tickled, "I don't know how she escaped. The recalcitrant ones are kept in the sun, but well chained. It's as if she knew there would be a gathering of royals. Came right for us."

On the way back to Kpembe, Wurche rode her horse, Baki, slowly, Mma sitting behind her. Mma complained if she did anything but walk like a snail.

"Salaga is ruined," said Mma. "I don't come often, but every time I do, it seems to be in worse shape than before. When I was a girl, you could drink water from the wells. Now, I'm sure even slaves don't want that water touching them. And that horrible woman who came at us ... I hate to say it, but when we were under the Asante, that would never have happened. They were more tactical in the way they managed Salaga. Since they were forced out we haven't built anything for ourselves. All we know is infighting."

Lost in her thoughts, Wurche grunted in response. Moro intrigued her. Was it the sharp symmetry of his face, the dark blue of his skin? Or was it because they had a shared past, one she couldn't even remember? She tried to conjure up images, but her memory was as dry as half the wells in Salaga. Then, as often happens, thoughts of the past led to thoughts of the future, a future she would soon have to contemplate, a future that was appearing more unpleasant by the day because everyone was pushing for her to get married. She'd managed to escape the drudgery of housework by convincing her father to let her study with a teacher in Salaga, but even so, things had stagnated. The next level was to begin teaching women about being a good Muslim, but she could only do that when she was married, which she didn't want. What she most desired was to help lead her people, the Gonjas. She hadn't been named Wurche for nothing. Queen. The original Wurche led a battalion of three hundred men to safety. That such a woman had existed two hundred years before she herself was born should give her hope. And what of Aminah of Zazzau, from an even earlier era, who refused to get married and killed her lovers to prevent anyone from usurping her throne? Aminah of Zazzau could do these things after her parents died. Wurche didn't want to lose her family, but was certain they would soon insist on her getting married. What would happen if she let them have their way, but only on the condition that she was allowed to choose? The general rule was royals married royals. What if she told them she'd chosen someone like Moro? A commoner. Maybe when he reached the status of Babatu, he'd be acceptable.

Back in Kpembe, Wurche dismounted Baki, helped Mma off, and led Baki into the stable. In the courtyard of Etuto's palace, a white man stood in front of Wurche's father and brothers. They were back more quickly than she'd expected.

Her father was seated on his ceremonial leopard skins, as one of the three lesser chiefs of Kpembe. Did it mean anything that the other two were absent? And these white men! She found them more bothersome and less impressive than others seemed to. Their shea butter hue suggested ill health and she could feel her distrust for them in her bones. And every week now, some new white man came to see Etuto and the other chiefs, offering friendship. Salaga, her father had explained, was strategic—the meeting point between forest and Sahel, and within reach of the confluences of the Nakambe and Daka rivers with River Adirri, which eventually emptied into the sea.

Guns, bottles of brown alcohol and bags of salt had been placed at Etuto's feet. Next to the white man and his entourage were four trussed-up sheep, a pile of yams and two large elephant tusks.

"Your people helped us shed the cruel yoke of the Asante," Etuto was saying, "and for that we are forever grateful, but Salaga has not been the same since."

"And *we* recognize the importance of Salaga," said the white man's interpreter, a tall man with no hair. "Which is why we want to find ways to help you. Salaga is an important town to all of us and we need to open it up to the coast. With your friendship and help, of course."

"The Asante stopped sending kola here after you defeated them," said Etuto. "We need kola nuts back in our markets in Salaga. The caravans will stop coming here if we don't have kola. If you want Salaga to prosper, bring kola."

In the past, the Gonjas and other nations nearby owed the Asante annual tribute in slaves. The slaves worked Asante farms or were sent to lands such as Dom Francisco de Sousa's Bahia. Then, the British defeated the Asante. When people in

Salaga heard about it, they slaughtered every Asante in town. After that, the Asante choked off Salaga from the kola trade and, according to Mma, the town had never recovered.

Wurche wiped the beads of sweat dotting her nose with the sleeve of her smock.

"The kola nut," Etuto said again.

After the visitors left, Wurche rushed past her brothers into Etuto's room. She wrapped her arms around her father, who stopped and soaked in the embrace. A bottle in her father's pocket poked her breastbone. She settled on a skin in the antechamber, waiting for him to go in and change. He came back out, uncapped the bottle, took a deep swig, and grimaced.

"Cheap." He cocked the bottle in Wurche's direction and she shook her head. A ritual, even though Wurche didn't drink.

"Why do you keep welcoming them?"

"Our situation is growing complicated. I need all the help I can get."

"Is this because of Kete-Krachi? Was it about who will succeed old Kpembewura?"

In the event of the old chief's death, succession would either go to the old Kpembewura's son Shaibu, to Etuto, or to another lesser chief. Each of them represented a different line of the royal family. Etuto's line had been sidelined for generations and from the looks of things, they would be once again. However, Etuto was convinced that if the white man helped him gain access to kola, he could restore Salaga to its glory and the other two lines would pick him as successor to the old Kpembewura.

"It's been a long day," he said. "We just got back and the British officers were already here. I need to rest. I promise to tell you about it tomorrow."

Wurche's brothers walked in, as if their father's words were the password they needed.

"Shouldn't we be working with our allies in Dagbon?" asked Wurche. "Instead of these white men. Or fix relations with the Asante?"

"What?" said Dramani. "The Asante who turned us into *their* slave raiders, making us raze entire villages to meet their yearly tributes?"

"At least we were still independent," said Wurche.

"How were we independent, when even our market was under Asante control?" said Dramani. He was always going on about how people shouldn't own other people and it was after one of those speeches that Mma had said he had a woman's spirit.

"People shift allies all the time," said Wurche. "We did it. There was a time when we were enemies with Dagbon. How many wars did we fight against each other? Now Etuto's best friends come from there. I trust the Asante more than the white men."

"Like Etuto mentioned," Sulemana said, "it's been a long day. Have you told her?"

"What?" asked Wurche.

"We're moving to the farm," he said gravely.

"Why?"

"I am tired," said Etuto.

"He says he needs a quiet place to think," added Dramani.

They only went to the farm once a year, for Etuto to rest. Drenched in boredom the day after they arrived, Wurche would begin counting down the days till they returned. There was nothing to do there. None of them farmed. Etuto's slaves tended the unfruitful land. And, unlike Kpembe, it didn't have a big town a fifteen-minute horse ride away. Something wasn't adding up. Why did they have to move, not just visit?

"Wurche," said Sulemana, "go and prepare the little ones."

She would tell Mma to prepare her younger siblings, and say Etuto requested it. She didn't understand children. They got in her way. They were unpredictable. And their mothers were still around. Her mother had been from the area around Etuto's farm, and the people there would not stop telling her how much she looked like this woman she had never had the chance to meet.

Aminah

Other caravans arrived in Botu, but none were as spectacular as the Sokoto caravans headed for Jenne. Baba often came back with a Salaga-bound caravan. The number of travelers in it had reduced more than ever, but because Baba could arrive with it, Na made them cook and sell.

Aminah approached each caravan with a belly tied in knots, frightened of encountering the man from the Sokoto caravan. She made sure the twins stayed at her side, and as they shouted out "Maasakokodanono" in their high-pitched, singsong voices, bits of their excitement punctured her nervousness. This excitement wasn't about newness; it was about hearing of Baba's adventures.

Others, too, were looking for familiar faces, even though some people didn't miss the chance to steal a glance at a pretty item or two; they searched for familiar clothes, although the people who went away always came back dressed in something that sparkled brighter, something that suggested they had left Botu; everyone's collective noses seemed to sniff for the smells of their loved ones, but the aromas of cooked food, new spices and novelty perfumes overwhelmed their senses. It was a fight between what the people of Botu knew and what was new. And, always, what they knew won. They wanted their fathers, mothers, brothers and sisters back.

For a month, Hassana, Husseina and Aminah stared and stared until the last beggar had paraded by. After another month, they started asking. No one had seen Baba and his albino donkey. The third month Baba was away, Na told them not to sell anything to the caravans. They had made enough from the previous months to survive, and Na said people would talk if they kept on as if everything was all right. The fifth month Baba was away, Na forbade her girls to wear black or cry in front of others. She said there was no reason to cry.

Aminah soon found that Na said things only so the neighbors would have nothing to talk about. Na, like Aminah, kept things buried in her belly and needed to be coaxed to let them out. One evening it had rained so hard that Aminah and Eeyah's roof caved in, so Aminah went into Na's room to sleep and Eeyah into Issa-Na's. Aminah was shocked to find tears streaming out of Na's eyes. Hassana and Husseina lay on the mat, Husseina curled along Na's spine, and Hassana rubbing Na's belly. It was only then that Aminah noticed that Na's belly was as large as the calabash Obado used to drink his millet wine. Her large smocks had hidden this very important detail.

"Why didn't you tell Baba about the baby?" said Aminah, remembering that when Issa was born, Baba had not done his caravan trip.

"It was too early," said Na. "It's still too early. I don't know if this baby will stay or not. Not every baby is meant for this earth. Sometimes, Otienu breathes a spirit into a body and realizes that he wants the spirit back. And that's the baby's destiny. But I tried to warn him. I felt it, that he shouldn't go, but do men listen?"

Every night, Aminah would return to Na's room and find her mother weeping. Aminah's own tears were right behind her breastbone, ready to flow in an unstoppable pool, but she remembered her father's last words to her, that she should take care of her mothers. Had he known he wouldn't be coming back?

The next day, she went to the neighbors and asked their son Motaaba to fix her bedroom roof. She dragged the twins out of Na's room, undid their cornrows, which were looking wilder than the grass around Botu, and sat Husseina on a stool between her knees.

"How did Na get the baby in her belly?" asked Husseina.

Aminah had some idea of how babies were made. Some of her friends were already married and had come back to Botu with their babies, so she knew it involved being with a man, but since she hadn't had a suitor yet, she hadn't been initiated into the ways of womanhood.

"It was a gift from Baba," she responded.

"Baba hasn't been here," retorted Hassana, arm's lengths away, drawing stick men and women in the sand. "And he's not coming back."

"Well, he gave it to her before he left," said Aminah. She turned to Hassana. "And we don't know that yet."

"Why didn't he give Issa-Na a gift?" asked Husseina.

Aminah wanted to have answers. She, too, had many questions. She wanted to know how babies were made. Why Baba married Na and then Issa-Na. Why Baba wasn't back. Why, if she was as beautiful as people claimed she was, she didn't have a suitor. Yet the person she could talk to was lost somewhere no one knew.

"Aminah, my question," said Husseina.

"Because she's the first wife, she gets the gift first. When Baba comes back, he'll give Issa-Na a gift too."

"Baba is not coming back," said Hassana.

"Why do you keep saying that?" asked Aminah.

"I dreamt that he was in a room with no doors and windows and he kept touching the walls to find a hole," said Hassana.

"So that was Baba," said Husseina. "I also dreamt that someone was stuck in a place with no light."

Even though it had happened a few times, Aminah wasn't sure if it was possible for the twins to dream of the same things. Usually, their shared dreams were of Botu or their friends at the water hole. Harmless things. There was something more sinister about this one.

"It doesn't mean he's not coming back," she said, more to reassure herself.

After she finished the twins' cornrows, she went to Issa-Na's room and was enveloped in grassy, minty air, from the medicinal herbs she gave to Issa to cure his many sicknesses. Ebony roots, baobab leaves, dawadawa bark, Issa-Na had it all. Issa-Na was teaching him to play awale, and was rattling the seeds in her hand over the wooden, round hollows of the board when Aminah walked in. Awale was Aminah's favorite game and others were often surprised at how competitive she got, trying to end up with four seeds in the most number of hollows. Issa waved at Aminah.

"I came to find out if I could help you with anything," said Aminah.

"No, thank you," said Issa-Na.

Aminah was about to walk out, when Issa-Na whispered, her voice a shaky version of itself, "You don't realize how much you love someone until they're gone. Maybe he ate something and fell sick. Maybe someone tried to cheat him and things went badly. He'd have sent word if he'd been able to. Or maybe he got lost. But the way he's quiet ... he probably would not have talked to anyone." Her hair had been tied back, but as she said this, she let it loose, and it grew like a cloud around her face, thick and full of tiny coils. In that moment, Aminah thought her beautiful. That she was teaching her son awale also warmed Aminah's heart.

"Let's keep praying," said Aminah.

As if released from a trance, Issa-Na realized who she was talking to and closed her mouth.

Aminah decided to talk to Eeyah the next evening. Everyone said the aged were wise. She would have answers. Usually, the old lady was knocked out before Aminah even entered the room, so Aminah finished cleaning the evening pots as fast as she could and went into the hut she shared with her grandmother.

Eeyah wiped her fallen breasts with a wrapper and made for her pipe, carefully folded in a piece of cloth next to the mat she shared with Aminah. From birth, Aminah had slept in her grandmother's room. Eeyah was the one who bathed her and looked after her. To allow Na and Baba time for each other, it made sense for the baby to stay with her grandmother. Eeyah took the pipe out of the cloth, held the bowl, and looked about for her tobacco leaves. She stuffed the leaves in the bowl of the pipe and suddenly seemed to notice Aminah for the first time.

"Is the fire still going?" she asked.

"Yes, Eeyah."

The old lady went out and shuffled back in with a lit pipe. She slit her eyes at Aminah. "Why are you here so early?" She extended her tongue and inserted the pipe into her mouth.

Aminah watched her grandmother while thinking up an answer. Baba must have looked more like his father. Where his eyes were round, Eeyah's were long and sharp. While Baba appeared perpetually distant, Eeyah looked like the kind of person you couldn't lie to. When Aminah was younger, her friends avoided their house because they said her grandmother was a witch.

"Is Baba still alive?" said Aminah.

"Oh my child. What a question," whispered Eeyah, pipe between her teeth. "Only Otienu knows." Eeyah's skin, which Aminah had always found beautiful, was beginning to lose its luster. The air was hot and heavy and left a wet sheen on everyone's skin but Eeyah's. Was her son's disappearance affecting her health?

"When I was a girl," continued Eeyah, "my baba would tell me about how people were kidnapped and sent up through a desert only to end up as slaves. Many of them didn't survive the terrible journey. Their bodies were often found next to wells. They died just as they reached a source of water. We didn't live in Botu then; we were closer to Jenne. He said he and his parents lived even farther away from Jenne, but because of raiders and people of the book, they moved down. Now the raiders come from down, not from up. Going to Jenne is safer than going to Salaga. But I pray ..."

"Eeyah, what are you saying?"

"Nothing, my child. Don't listen to my ramblings. But hear this, we don't know if and when he'll show up. But whatever happens, you need to be strong. There are people who need to be taken care of, and there are people who take care of others. You are your mother's daughter. She takes care of people, as do you. But with the baby she's carrying, she's more likely than not going to break down. We all know Issa-Na can barely take care of herself. It's only a matter of time before *I* join the ancestors. It's on you to be strong for us all. It's not an easy task I'm asking you to take on. It will absorb a lot of your energy. You already do so much for the house. And it will be a drain on here too." She jabbed at Aminah's heart. "But we need someone to look up to, and that person is you, with all your fifteen years. We have no choice. *You* have no choice."

Eeyah set down her pipe, tugged Aminah into her arms, and began a song she'd always sung. One that only then made sense to Aminah. It was a sad song about their people leaving a land in the East, where a long river made the land fertile and provided so much food there was surplus, and how invaders had forced them out, making them travel the desert, eventually disintegrating them into smaller and smaller clans.

Wurche

A small forest marked the lower boundary of Etuto's farm and next to it was a water hole. At the upper end, the soil grew drier and stonier. The sparse land of the farm stretched on forever, and yet, the feeling one got there was not unlike being cornered in a small, dark room. Wurche's boredom and claustrophobia were aggravated by the dreams she kept having of the slave-raiding Moro. Her father hadn't come out of his room in days, and his wives wove in and out, each time looking more perplexed than before they went in, sometimes clutching empty bottles of alcohol. There was no telling when or if the family would return to Salaga-Kpembe. Every so often, Etuto slid into one of these episodes: days when he did nothing but apparently stare at the wall. The rumor was that he'd stop eating and bathing, and wouldn't speak to anyone while the bout lasted, occasionally drinking rum or gin. Mma, always full of explanations, said it was jinns that possessed him. In his lucid moments, he'd asked that Wurche never be allowed to see him like that.

She mounted Baki and rode in the direction of Salaga. She could say her teacher had sent a messenger for her. Or that Mma—Wurche would toy with her forgetfulness—had left something behind. She was so occupied with finding an excuse for leaving that she almost missed Dramani wiping down a musket in the grass, a pouch slung across his chest. Covered with a brown patina, its inscription in Arabic was still visible. One of Etuto's first guns with his name on it. A wide smile lit up Dramani's face, as it always did when he saw her. People who didn't know better thought they were twins, a resemblance she refused to see. They were born a day apart, to different mothers. Dramani's mother was still going in and out of Etuto's hut; Wurche wondered if her mother would have done the same.

"Who gave you that?" she asked, not returning his smile.

"Etuto," said Dramani. "He insists that I improve my shooting to be a man."

Sulemana was the only one who had a gun. Wurche wanted to go to Etuto's room to protest his partiality. True, she didn't have a manhood to prove, but she'd asked him many times. Sulemana had allowed his siblings to shoot his musket a few times and Wurche proved better than Dramani every time. Etuto knew that. Yet she wasn't being given a chance. Also, the white men had given Etuto so many guns that he hadn't used. He could have given them each one. Then she had another thought.

"Are we shooting at guinea fowl now?" she asked. "What happened to the trusty bow and arrow?"

Dramani was quiet.

"Shouldn't you be learning how to grow yam?"

"Perhaps," he said after a while.

"You're hiding something." It was quite possible that Etuto was grooming Dramani, since he wanted to rest, but one is often suspicious for good reason. There had to be more to this story of Dramani being given a gun.

"Shall we work this together?" asked Dramani.

He was the last person with whom she wanted to spend her afternoon, but shooting would be a way of avoiding trouble. She nodded and waited as he scrambled back to the stable to get his horse. They rode out silently to the small forest, redolent of dust and cinnamon. Wurche dismounted and tied Baki to a tree. The trees were spaced wide enough for her to keep an eye on Baki and for them to practice comfortably and not scare the horses. The sun's rays sliced through the branches between the tall trees, splaying out onto the dry, gray soil. Dramani thrust the musket into Wurche's hands too happily, and she, just as willingly, took it.

Now that she'd thought of it, guinea fowl *would* be delicious targets, but the soil on the farm was so arid, all the birds had fled. She looked about and saw, about ten paces ahead, a slim truncated tree. She found dried baobab pods, most of which dissolved to powder in her hands. She dropped the large stone she'd considered—the shot would ricochet badly—and settled for a short branch, which she placed on top of the trunk. She went back to Dramani.

"Where's the cartridge?" she said. "I hope you brought a lot."

Dramani frantically rooted through his leather pouch and took out a small cartridge wrapped in a paper and a tiny clay pot—the kind Mma liked to carry around filled with shea butter so her skin was always shiny. Nerves hit Wurche suddenly. She'd been confident all along, but she'd only practiced with Sulemana a few times—two or three—and an expert that did not make. Still, she took the items from Dramani and proceeded as if she were. She bit open the paper cartridge, revealing the gunpowder, as black as Baki's coat, and poured it into the musket's barrel. She extracted the ball from the cartridge, slathered it in shea butter, pushed it down the barrel, and added the rest of the gunpowder and the rest of the cartridge. She took the rod and tapped down the barrel's contents, cocked the musket over her shoulder, and tried to ignore Dramani's nervous rasping next to her as she aimed at the branch. She homed in and pulled the trigger. Nothing happened.

"Are you sure you loaded everything correctly?" Dramani asked. Her brother wasn't a vicious person. His question was free of guile. Someone else—such as Wurche herself—would have asked the same question and laced it with impatience. "You didn't open the lock."

That was what ignited the whole thing.

"I forgot," she whispered, as she popped open the lock.

She poured gunpowder into the exposed chamber and as she was closing the lock, a loud bang and dusty plume issued from the musket, which she dropped in fright. As far away as she was, Baki whinnied.

"Are you hurt?" asked Dramani.

"No."

She picked up the musket again.

"We can stop if it's unsafe. These things are terrible. We should be able to take care of a nation without them. And I shouldn't have to prove that I'm a man with it."

"If we had no weapons, we would be just like the people who end up in the Salaga market. It's the way the world has always worked. You can have ideas, but you need a way to get them through. And unfortunately, the way is through force. It's why we have jihads. Jaji said it was the same with the Christians. The prophet they call Issa. His teachings were all about peace. But the only way his message spread was through the Crusades, which were very violent. Ah, even closer. The Asante. They became so powerful because they were a military people. If we want to keep our people united, we need to have as many weapons as possible and we need to know how to use them well."

"But it means you think people shouldn't have the right to choose what they want. You have to force them to bend *your* way."

"If people knew what they wanted, we royals wouldn't exist. You wouldn't have all the benefits of being Etuto's son. You wouldn't even have time to be sitting around pondering such questions. You would be sweating on a farm as unproductive as the ones around here. Now let's try this weapon."

"What *is* Jaji's name? You've always called her Jaji. Teacher. Why not Hajia? She has been to Mecca, no?"

"Dramani, these questions give me the sense that you don't want to shoot. If you want Etuto to take you seriously, you have to learn. You can't give up after failing the first time."

She started again, this time pouring the gunpowder into the lock's compartment before adding the rest of the ammunition. She aimed and shot at the branch. The musket ball knocked the branch off the stump, and she felt like jumping up and down in victory. She passed the musket to Dramani.

"You have a natural skill for these things," he said.

"What use is it to have a skill no one appreciates?"

"I do."

"Just shoot."

A week later, after another shooting session, Wurche and Dramani came upon Sulemana bathing in the water hole near the forest. Wurche wanted to scare him, but he saw them and waved them over.

"I see you less on this small farm than I do in Kpembe," she said.

"Life is strange," Sulemana said, treading water. "One can get lost in small spaces. And in big places, one feels not so lost. I know you don't like being here."

"At least Dramani is letting me shoot his musket. Tell us what is going on. No one is farming, Etuto is not coming out of his room, something is happening, and no one is telling me anything."

"You know his illness," said Sulemana.

"When he gets better, will we go back?" asked Wurche. Sulemana shrugged, dropping his hands in the water with a loud splash. "We can't live on this barren farm for eternity. Sulemana, please tell me something!"

"Fine, but you didn't hear this from me. Dramani, you too. All I can say is he's better, but he's been talking a lot about you, Wurche."

"Now you're lying. Nothing in the last three weeks has had anything to do with me. If he'd thought about me, he'd have given me a gun, too."

"I'm sorry," said Sulemana, splashing water at both of them. "I can't say any more."

A few days later, Wurche began to put the pieces together. She awoke to find the women of the farm sitting behind mounds of guinea fowl, pinching off their polka-dotted feathers to expose dark pink meat. Others were pounding groundnuts. Several women of the farm sat behind pots of tuo. Mma was talking about how nice it would be to have a baby in the household again as she tugged on the tufts of a little bird. When it was naked of its feathers, she set it on a board and hacked it to pieces. Wurche found it odd that her grandmother went from talking about a baby to hacking at a tiny creature. Mma stood up creakily, counted on her fingers, stared at the carcasses of plucked guinea fowl, whispered something to another aunt, and gleamed. Mma lived for these moments—when she could prove how well brought up she was.

When Wurche was younger, Mma thought it would be good for her granddaughter to take part in the household chores, especially since Wurche didn't have a mother who would naturally have included her in such tasks. Wurche had overheard Mma saying that even if Wurche's mother had survived childbirth, *she* Mma, would still have had to train Wurche. Wurche had wondered what that meant. Mma spent weeks showing her how to keep a kitchen: what the different cuts of poultry were, how to buy beef and mutton and goat, how to boil rice so it came out in nice individual grains versus how to boil rice so the whole meal clumped together to make rice tuo, how to find the best cures in the bush, how to wash clothes, how to fold clothes, who could straighten clothes the best in Kpembe, how to get rid of odors in the washroom. What Wurche gleaned from all that work was that it was designed to please a husband. Those weeks were excruciating and made her despise women for putting such effort into things men probably didn't even notice. Now, Wurche surmised that all this food preparation had to be related to a man. Her father? What could he be celebrating, given that he had spent the last weeks staring at the wall of his room? He had young children around the house—how many she couldn't say—so another would be too much. Wurche was curious, but she knew the moment she stuck in her nose, she'd regret it; Mma would put a knife in her hand and set her to work. So she kept her distance, slid around the curve of her room and made for her father's hut, where a small group of women moiled about, whispering and tying and retying the scarves around their heads. She'd never

seen these people and because of their number, she was sure
Etuto would have no time to answer her questions.

She went for a swim to cool her chest, then settled for a
nap under the closest tree. She dreamt she was a child again.
Sulemana flung her in the air and caught her as her chest erupted
into giggles. He hugged her, and that's when she realized he
wasn't Sulemana at all, but Moro. Grown-up Moro. It had an
instant sobering effect and woke her up. She hugged herself.
The sun had warmed her skin, but it pocked, as if a cold wind
had wafted by. She didn't know how much time had passed,
but when she saw Mma slugging towards her, she guessed it
might be late.

Mma sat down by Wurche, whispering "Ay, Allah, my knees."
Then to Wurche she said, "Your father bought you a new
smock." Perhaps Dramani had told Etuto that she'd wanted a
gun too and he thought this was a more appropriate gift for her.

"Who were those people outside Etuto's hut?" asked Wurche.

"You're just meeting him," said Mma calmly. Why wasn't
Mma answering her question? Or had she? Then it dawned
on her: another suitor. They had never cooked so much food
for any of her other wooers. A different kind of suitor, then.

"You haven't learned your lessons. This will go nowhere."

"You'll like him," Mma said, placing her palm on Wurche's
shoulder.

Another suitor. Despite her words, Wurche wasn't convinced
it would be like the others, that it would go nowhere. Something
was different.

Wurche had learned that European kings sat on thrones.
The Asante kings sat on stools. Gonja kings and chiefs sat on
skins. When you were made king, you were enskinned—given
lion and leopard hides. The higher you were, the more power

you had, the more sophisticated your animal skin. Said to have been sat on by Namba, Gonja's founding father, the skins of the Kpembe king were prized. Etuto sat on leopard skins, which had now been laid out in the farmhouse's courtyard. They were surrounded by a spread of mats woven in greens, reds, yellows and indigos, and leather poufs were plopped in every corner. The women outside Etuto's hut were fluffing pillows, straightening mats, setting down bowls of kola. The children of the farm jumped from pouf to pouf until Mma appeared and shooed them away. The slip of Wurche's new silk smock was so smooth, she felt as if she were wearing nothing. She missed the itch of her normal smocks and especially the worn smell of the ones she liked to wear the most.

"You're worse than a wall gecko," Mma often said to her, because geckos always went back to the same place.

Mma, noticing Wurche, rushed over to her, scooped a vial of kohl from between her breasts, and started applying it to Wurche's eyes. She then doused her in a fragrance both holy and lucky because, its vendor said, it had come all the way from Mecca.

"You look beautiful," said Mma. Wurche felt naked. And strangely afraid.

By evening, Etuto and his advisors, sons and the other men of the family had filled half the courtyard, and the women had taken over the other. Every time Wurche tried to make her way to Etuto, someone would waylay her to greet a relative she didn't know existed. Her mother's grandfather's nephew. A distant aunt, who burst into tears because she said Wurche looked just like her mother. The woman had cried and pressed Wurche to her chest three times. These encounters always started with the question, "Do you know me?" Of course, she didn't, and she wanted to tell them to stop wasting her time, but the expectant, insistent look in their eyes—you *should* know me—would amuse her. So instead, she'd consider the person and consider their question, and land somewhere between a nod and a shake of her head. The person would then decide for themselves that Wurche was too young, or perhaps hadn't been born at that time, and only then would they let her go.

As for Etuto, he was flanked between two women to whom he kept whispering. His face was lit up by the bonfire and every time he leaned in the women giggled. He didn't look like a man who had spent the last weeks in a well with no light.

Wurche's mother had grown up in a hut about ten minutes away from Etuto's farm. Mma had never told her who her mother was, but over the years, she'd stitched together bits and concluded that her mother was not a royal and probably not a wife. "Concubine" was probably the best word. Like one of the women sitting by Etuto. Then it hit her: if her mother's people had been summoned—they had come in their numbers—whatever was happening was a foregone conclusion. This was a premarriage ceremony.

"Wurche," Etuto shouted, startling her, waving her over. As she drew closer, one of the women jumped off to make space. Wurche took her time to sit down. He lowered his voice. "You're not happy, I know."

Wurche stared at the breasts of the woman sitting by her father; they drooped like baobab pods.

"Are you better?" she asked.

"Much better. I'm sorry I haven't had time to sit with you, to explain what is going on," Etuto said. "It's this nasty business of who inherits the skin to become chief of Kpembe and Salaga. Our family has been left out for far too long. You're doing me

... not just me, but our entire Kanyase line, a favor. The other times you had suitors we didn't need the alliance, so when you said no I didn't push you. But you will like this young man."

Wurche thought of the times Etuto himself had told her that Gonja princesses were the luckiest women in the world: they got to choose their partners, even if the men were already married. Now, she was being denied this privilege. Her mouth grew dry. And why was everyone insisting she'd like the young man? They barely understood her, and were sure to misunderstand the kind of man she would appreciate.

"We have to deal with hard realities, Wurche," Etuto continued. "War is coming. I moved here so I could prepare our strategy." Even as he said this, his face remained pleasant. Etuto seemed a happy man. Wurche couldn't imagine him just staring at the wall when his sickness came or being at war with anyone. But her hunch was right too. Her father was not resting. "You were even the one who even gave me the idea," he continued. "That we should focus on our friendship with Dagbon. An alliance with Dagbon is the only way we'll make it out of this situation whole. They are well armed, and they like me because my sister married one of them. Marriage ensures that we'll treat each other with respe—"

Lunga beats drowned out Etuto's voice.

"Ah, they are here," Etuto boomed, hoisting himself up. He was a large man with dark skin that glistened in the bonfire glow. Everyone stood. "Dagbon has some of the finest drummers in the world. Listen."

He signaled for his men to head to the entrance. Four boys whirled, beating their lungas in a frenzy and churning up dust as they approached the entryway. Etuto and his men parted for the players. They were followed by a group of women ululating and clapping. Then in came three men, all similarly dressed in fine navy-striped smocks, black embroidered riding boots, and white scarves draped on their shoulders. The women stopped and clapped at the one in the middle. When the drumming died down, Etuto led the new arrivals to their skins.

The man at the center of attention also had a round face, but where Etuto was tall, he was wide. He looked soft. Wurche glanced at her suitor and decided to study her fingernails. He was nothing like Moro. He was, in many ways, his exact opposite. Even his skin color paled. It didn't run deep and luminous like Moro's. She had hoped for a miracle. She had brought this on herself. In the future, she had to insert herself into the advice she gave her father.

Trays of wagashie and calabashes of millet beer were passed around. Etuto strode to the prince from Dagbon and they exchanged what must have been uproarious words, because they both burst into loud laughter. Etuto placed his left palm on the prince's back and took him to greet the men of the household, then the women, old ladies first. Then, they stopped before Wurche.

"May I present my daughter," said Etuto. "Wurche, this is Prince Adnan, the chief of Dagbon's handsome nephew."

Wurche shook the man's soft hands. If this made Etuto happy, she'd do it for him. And then she could ask for what she wanted.

Aminah

Aminah wanted to do everything for Na and the new baby. She bathed the baby; she carried her on her back, lulling her to sleep; she learned to distinguish the good baby burps and farts from the bad ones; she stayed up with Na, keeping shifts and helping to feed the baby's insatiable appetite. And while she was grieving Baba's absence, it didn't stop her from enjoying what a sponge the baby was, the way she looked about and imitated the faces she saw around her, and how sometimes her own expressions burst forth from her blood. It was uncanny how much she looked like Baba. The lazy way her eyes opened and closed. Everyone saw but no one said.

Time passed. The baby started holding her neck up and attempting speech, little gurgles of coughs that brought some laughter to the household. She put everything in her mouth, and Hassana loved nothing more than having the baby gnaw on her nose with her toothless gums. These were the little moments that kept the family going. The baby filled the gap Baba's absence had ripped open, even though signs of him were still everywhere: an abandoned shoe in the courtyard looking like a mouth agape; a patch he'd badly repaired above the kitchen door; the lingering smell of patchouli and leather outside his room; his donkey's trough collecting dust and grass.

A good man, everyone repeated, when they came to see the women. Each time Aminah tried to remember his face, the image was faded, less sharp. His reddish skin, his hesitant smile, his large eyes that took in everything and judged nothing; these details had lost luster. She hadn't been able to go into his workroom. None of them had, more than a year later. Aminah imagined it cobwebbed, a hill of sand over his work, a place in need of cleaning, but she didn't have the heart to enter the space. If she went in, the solid wall she'd built over days, weeks, months, would crumble faster than an anthill in a storm. They were carrying on fine and had to keep going.

Aminah often tidied Na's room, but hadn't touched the clothes Baba had left behind, still in the neat pile atop the stool he would sometimes sit on after working on his shoes. Whenever Baba had come in and sat there, Aminah used to excuse herself. Between making shoes and taking care of two wives, he surely hadn't gotten many moments to soak in time with Na. She imagined Na starting off the conversation with, "You know what Rama-Na told me today?"; "You know where Adjaratu-Na went this morning?"; "You know how Motaaba-Na cooks her neri soup?" The woman would launch into rich, nonstop detail, while Baba just listened, lovingly absorbing the dimples that appeared and hid in Na's cheeks as she talked. Theirs, Aminah was convinced, was a great friendship, one with no secrets. Na's family, a group of cattle herders, had always moved around. They were passing through Botu when Baba espied a young Na milking a cow. By the time he worked up the nerve to ask for her hand in marriage, her family had moved north. Luckily, it was in the dry season, and Baba was able to find her after three days by using green patches where the cows would be sent to graze as his guides.

Aminah watched the baby sucking greedily on Na's breast as her mother stared up at the ceiling.

"Na," said Aminah, snapping her mother out of her daze.

"I knew you were here. Sorry, I was just thinking ..."

"About what?"

"Nothing in particular."

"Motaaba's father just came back from Jenne."

Na watched her daughter with surprised, expectant eyes. It was cruel to make her mother think she was bearing news about Baba, so Aminah immediately explained. "Motaaba-Na said he brought her more than enough salt, so we were welcome to come for some."

"That's kind of her," said Na, sending the baby's mouth to her other breast.

"Should I go and get some?"

Na paused. "I did a sacrifice to bring back Baba," she said suddenly. "I know we are supposed to accept whatever happens to us as Otienu's plan for our spirits, as our destinies, but it's easy to say and preach things. Life is never clean. I can't accept that Baba's destiny was to come into our lives and disappear without a trace. I've been so lost. I didn't know what else to do, so I consulted with Eeyah and Obado. We gave Obado an old ram and he slit its throat. When you started talking about Jenne, I thought ... I'd hoped the parli had worked." Her voice grew thin.

"I'm sorry, Na ..."

"We have to stay strong." She hawked the phlegm in her throat. "Get some of Motaaba's father's salt. Tell Motaaba-Na she is welcome to come for whatever she wants in exchange."

Issa-Na brought Obado and a slight, nervous man with duiker-like eyes to the house one afternoon. The clouds were fat and gray, the air was charged and hot, and everyone prayed for rain.

"The house of women," said Obado, settling on a mat Aminah set down for him. "See how respectful she is," he said to the small man.

A gust of wind blew Obado's cap off, exposing his bald patch. Hassana ran to catch the cap and, in a show of false attentiveness, placed it back on his head.

The family sat around and the baby observed the duiker man, aware that his was a new presence. Aminah fetched water for the guests and missed the beginning of Obado's speech, but when she got back he was saying their community was like a flock of birds.

"And so we need to work in groups, otherwise we are vulnerable. Our brother, your father,"—he paused and inhaled deeply—"has been gone from us for over a year now. And so when this fine gentleman, our own Issa-Na's uncle, came to ask for my blessing, I couldn't refuse, because this house needs a man, the way plants need water. Issa-Na's uncle would like to ask for Aminah's hand in marriage. Issa-Na said her husband and *your* husband, Aminah-Na, had been talking about marrying Aminah for a while and would have arranged a marriage on his return."

Obado's words felt like a punch to Aminah's belly. Did Na know about this? Eeyah? Aminah stole a glance at Eeyah, puffing on the pipe between her teeth. She seemed unbothered. Issa-Na was beaming. Had she and Baba planned this all along? The moment was awkward but everyone was carrying on as if nothing outrageous was happening. The only person who appeared to share Aminah's confusion was Na, who was bouncing her baby overenthusiastically on her lap. Aminah stared at her mother until their eyes met, and Na raised her eyebrows, as if to ask what Aminah's move would be. Just as Obado was saying there was plenty of time to plan the wedding, the rain clouds burst. Na rushed to her room with the baby and Aminah followed.

Na lowered herself onto her mat and wiped the raindrops off the baby.

"Is it true, what they said?" asked Aminah.

Na didn't answer immediately, then said, "The important question is, do you want to do this? Don't worry about the rest of us."

"I want what you have with Baba." *I want what you* had *with Baba.* Neither sentence sounded right. Na said nothing. "I don't mean to disrespect her," continued Aminah, "but Issa-Na is lying about Baba wanting to marry me off. He would have said something to you ... or to me."

Na shook her head sadly. Her silence was telling another story, suggesting that Aminah had perhaps thought wrongly about her parents' intimacy. It made her wonder ... if her parents had had the great friendship she'd envisaged, would Baba have married Issa-Na? Aminah's belly told her that even if it was at his family's insistence, quiet, stubborn Baba would have had his way. So *he* had chosen Issa-Na.

"Don't do anything," Na said. "I will talk to him and tell him it's in our nature to think things through and not rush to a decision. In a fortnight, I'll send Issa-Na to bring him back and when he comes we'll be so unreasonable with our demands, he'll think twice about his request."

Aminah was pleased that, despite her misery, Na hadn't lost her fire.

Issa-Na went to her village to fetch her uncle, as Na requested. She left Issa behind because the journey was long and would take its toll on his already weak body. Sleeping arrangements changed: Na slept in her room with the baby; Eeyah shared her room with Husseina; and Hassana (who said Eeyah's snores kept her awake), Issa and Aminah slept in Issa-Na's room. Issa had started carrying himself with more confidence. His back stood erect, as if his mother's absence allowed him to mushroom into his rightful place: man of the house. Aminah took him to the farm to work, and he was helpful, his small hands dropping seeds faster than everyone else.

A week later Issa-Na was still away. Eeyah was telling the story of the mischievous spider that loved to outsmart everyone, especially the king, but stopped midway and said she'd tell the rest the next day. Aminah didn't like stories cut in half, but the baby had fallen asleep and she had to get her into bed before someone woke her again. She carried her into Na's room, where Na was lying, arms spread like bat's wings, her eyes fixed on the ceiling. She sat up, sniffled, and tried to wipe her eyes casually before reaching for the baby. Na set her down and wouldn't look at Aminah, who suddenly grew irritated, wondering why she was mourning so much for a man who kept secrets from her.

"Maybe Issa-Na and Obado are right," said Aminah. "We need to accept that Baba's gone, mourn him, and give the baby a name. Is she going to be nameless forever?"

Na shot a look that could have scorched Aminah's soul.

Aminah stood up, mumbled an apology and walked out, wishing she'd been less flippant. She strode in a path of blue moonlight, feeling more ashamed by the minute. She wanted to take a long walk, but the grass was wilder than it had ever been, so she sat on a rock outside the house and let her shame wash over her. She burst into tears, tears she'd held in for so long. They flowed and threatened not to stop. Then she prayed for Baba. That if he was still alive, he'd make his way back to them, especially for Na's sake. That if he wasn't, he'd made a safe journey to the ancestors. That the family could go on without him.

She didn't fall asleep easily that night. Hassana kicked every time Aminah shifted to find a comfortable position. When she was shaken awake not long after she had fallen asleep, she thought she had been tossing and turning again. Then unfamiliar sounds grew louder. Horses neighed. People screeched. There was wailing, crackling, a steady *clop-clop-clop* that grew louder outside the window. Hassana and Issa were awake too. It was too dark to read their expressions, but Aminah could feel them sitting up, too scared to move.

"Wait here." She peeked into the courtyard. Eeyah and Husseina were outside. Above the rooftop of the entrance, an orange dome blared, lighting up the sky as if the village were a massive bonfire. Aminah joined Husseina and Eeyah. Houses right next to theirs erupted in flame. The *clop-clop-clop* grew immediate. Issa and Hassana ran outside. The family made for Na's hut, but a horse burst through the entrance with a rider dressed in black, billowing clothing. He seemed to be floating on air, a winged figure with a roaring fire behind him. He swivelled a long-barrelled gun above his head, in a display that would have dazzled at another time and place, but in that moment made Aminah want to cower under a rock. He knocked Eeyah down with the barrel, pointed the muzzle at the children, and commanded them towards the entrance. Issa stood rooted, shaking. Aminah picked him up and grabbed Hassana's wrist. Hassana took Husseina's hand.

"No one else is here," Aminah shouted, frantic, desperate, hoping they'd leave their huts alone, not sure if they even spoke the same language. If she could save anyone, she wanted it to be Na and the baby.

The horsemen left Eeyah, who was not moving, and herded the children outside, where several other horsemen were leading people out of their homes. They rounded up everyone and roped them, one to the other, at the waist, mixing up men, women, girls, boys. It didn't matter. Families were torn apart, tied up with other families. Aminah put Issa down and gripped his hand, securing her hold on Hassana's wrist at the same time. She knew she was hurting them, but she needed to keep them together. All around, people cried, begged. Aminah looked back at the house; Na and the baby still hadn't come out. She was relieved, because the baby wouldn't survive the rough treatment. Aminah hoped Na was sleeping deeply, as she was wont to do sometimes. If she heard the commotion, she would surely come out.

The horsemen went around setting fire to rooftops. Others whipped the captives with fly whisks, yelling at them to move fast. Aminah looked back and still no one came from their compound. Had Na chosen not to come out?

The captives trooped single file, and when Aminah looked back, the whole village was engulfed in flames. Above them, the sky was cool and blue and indifferent, the moon haloed by wisps of white cloud. Aminah prayed Eeyah would wake up and rescue Na and the baby. A huge piece of char flew into the sky. The bright red fire ate everything, the smoke choked them, burned their eyes, and suddenly Aminah wasn't sure if being left behind was a blessing. She walked in a daze, unable to process what was going on. Something bad had happened, something bad was happening.

Issa tripped, Aminah tripped over him and Hassana fell with them. Then Husseina tripped over Aminah. The horsemen had helpers. They lashed at Aminah's shins, which got her on her feet. She straightened and helped Issa stand.

The village was burning up. They felt the heat even after the tallest tree appeared to be the size of a small branch. Nothing would survive a fire like that. Aminah choked up. Why had she been foolish? She should have woken Na. Tears made everything ahead watery. She couldn't see where her feet landed. Had Na and the baby and Eeyah survived? She retched when she thought of them burning to death. People sniveled and sobbed and whimpered. The crickets sang their same song: *Kreee-kreee-kreee.*

Wurche

She awaited her wedding day with dread, like a slave waiting to be sold, sure the day would come, but not knowing when it would be. And Wurche was angry. When she asked for details she was only told it had to be an auspicious date. She didn't like the man who had been presented to her, and who had already delivered the customary twelve pieces of kola to ask for her hand. Her anger, however, was not directed at Etuto and Mma, who had planned this; it was directed at herself, at how powerless she had let herself become. Even though she had agreed to marry the Dagomba prince, she still thought of ways to sabotage the wedding. Running away was the best way, but each plot she came up with crumbled like a moth-eaten smock when picked apart. Still, they gave her hope.

Her first plan was to move in with her mother's family, not too far from the farm. But they were the ones, more than anyone else, who wanted Wurche married. Every day, people who claimed to be her aunts came to Etuto's farm and mostly sat, waiting for the wedding day to be announced. The rabid glaze in their eyes when food was passed around suggested that they were so grateful to be connected to a royal family with resources (even if their main link, Wurche's mother, was no longer there) that there was no way they would betray Etuto.

If ever she tried going there, they would tie her up faster than lightning and return her to Etuto.

Her second plan was to run away to Asante. In her childhood, Mma had scared her so much with the idea of being sent to the Asante that she'd never overcome the fear of the short forest dwellers who would eat you without blinking. Mma said their cannibalism had made them the strongest kingdom in the region. But in truth the Asante grew strong because they controlled gold and kola, they had a king who could not be overthrown as easily as the Gonja kings, and the dense forest they lived in protected them from enemies even as strong as the British. Knowing all this didn't allay her fears: fear sank its roots deep. Still, it would be the perfect place to go, but she didn't speak their language and she would miss the spread of the savanna. She couldn't have a horse in the forest. Also, once it was discovered that she was from Salaga-Kpembe, and that she was a princess, they would probably behead her.

So she succumbed to her initial idea that her agreeing to the marriage could be used to barter with her father: she would ask for an active role in ruling. But then the old Kpembe king died, and events happened faster than Wurche could have predicted.

A large group of women had gathered outside Etuto's hut. It was magical, the way they appeared, like flies around a piece of fish, out of nowhere and in such numbers. Their individual voices were low, but collectively made a loud buzzing. One woman began to moan, and the moan became a scream.

"Wo yo!"

"Wo yo!"

"Wo yo!"

Wurche was convinced none of these women had even seen the Kpembe chief, and yet they were mourning him like they'd lost their children. Wurche found Mma dabbing her eyes. Not her too, she thought, but Mma had an explanation.

"He was the gum that held together our twin towns of Kpembe and Salaga, and the three lines competing for the skin. Now, the lines are divided on who will succeed him. I told you before—this will only create trouble. And the old Kpembewura was like a brother to me. He and your grandfather were very close. He was a good man."

A group of men, most of them with great white beards, arrived on their horses, jumped off and strode into Etuto's room, some even shoving the women out of their way. Wurche stole the chance to follow them in the flurry. She caught Mma's eyes as Mma reached out to stop her, but she was faster than her grandmother and slid into the hut.

Inside, the men settled down in circles, those already seated fanning themselves with their whisks. Wurche saw Sulemana and Dramani and made her way toward them. She could feel stares piercing her body with disapproval. An older man wagged his finger at her. She sat by Sulemana, who shook his head at her and laughed. Etuto watched through puffy eyes, waiting for everyone to settle. He made eye contact with her, frowned briefly and then his gaze moved on. He seemed a man with a lot more on his mind than his rebellious daughter. She didn't know what would happen with the Kpembewura dead, but it couldn't be good for Etuto's health. She looked around and saw Mma limp in, holding a gourd. She ambled in Wurche's direction.

"It was too fast," said one of the men to his neighbor. "Now, with this vacuum, vultures are already swooping in."

"We are not equipped for war," the neighbor responded.

The men's whispers grew louder, and in walked Etuto's mallam, the person whose advice counted the most. Etuto helped the old man onto the cow skin next to him, leaned in and whispered. Then he cleared his throat loudly, hushing the room. Mma had no choice but to sit down where she was; an immense relief for Wurche, because the old woman would have dragged her out.

"May the Kpembewura rest in peace," said Etuto.

"Ami," echoed the men in response. "Ami, Ami, Ami."

"Here is what is going to happen," continued Etuto. "We will head back to Kpembe in a day to meet the other Kanyase line elders to select the person who will be the next Kpembewura. We will then present the Lepo and Singbung lines with our chosen leader. Our line has been skipped for too many generations now, and when our kingdom was established, our great founder, Namba, left Kpembe to his three sons: Kanyase, Lepo, and Singbung. One was supposed to inherit the skin, then the next, then the third. Why then have two taken over and left out one? Why have we been sidelined? There have been four Lepo chiefs and three Singbung chiefs for the last seven skins. Not a single Kanyase chief. Some people say that Lepo and Kanyase were twins, and so were counted as one, which is why succession has always gone to Singbung and Lepo, but this is wrong. Kpembe was left to all three of us."

The men murmured among themselves.

"May the Kpembewura rest in peace," said a man across from Etuto. "I will support you becoming Kpembewura, although I come with unfortunate news. Before we left Salaga, the other lines claimed the skin should go, not to you, not to Prince Shaibu, who has himself said he wants no part in being

Kpembewura, but to Prince Nafu, because he has wealth. And at this time, we need the resources to rebuild Kpembe and Salaga."

"Nafu doesn't know the first thing about ruling," said another.

"Nafu is not interested in uniting us," Wurche said under her breath. "All he wants is to keep growing richer."

"Wealth or not," said Etuto, "the injustice has to stop. Three lines inherit the skin and we have to set right the balance on which our kingdom was founded."

"What if the other lines don't agree to our proposal?" asked the old man who had shaken his finger at Wurche.

"We have to get *our* people to agree first," whispered Sulemana. "That's the bigger struggle. But I think we're all afraid to acknowledge that our own people might say no."

"Then we will turn to our allies in Dagbon," said Etuto in response to the old man. Wurche looked about. Everyone was focused on him. She realized that going to Dagbon meant her wedding was imminent. "My daughter once made an astute observation. She said our lines are like the cooking pots our women use: unstable on two legs, perfect on three. The two lines have become corrupt without our input. And we've grown content with playing a ceremonial role."

Wurche's fear was briefly replaced with glee, but disappeared when Etuto's messenger burst into the room, his clothes swallowing his emaciated body, looking as if he'd been dragged in dust and beaten. He nodded before the gathering and prostrated himself before Etuto, who gave him permission to get up. He panted and whispered to Etuto. Etuto's mouth dropped open, but he gathered himself and thanked the messenger, who bowed and moved to the back of the room.

Etuto turned to his mallam and conferred with him before facing the group.

"We have to act quickly," he said gravely. "My messenger was on his way to Kpembe to deliver the news of our intended meeting to the other Kanyase leaders, when he met one of his trusted friends. His friend told him that not far off were soldiers being sent by the Singbung and Lepo families to attack us because they think we are plotting against them. Once they finish me off, they *will* install Prince Nafu as Kpembewura. The Lepo and Singbung lines are backing him and the other Kanyase leaders have declared me a rebel. Now, my friends, we are not well armed here. We have to leave for Dagbon as soon as possible. They'll come here and find no one. When we get to Dagbon, we'll finesse our strategy. Get the women to prepare. Thank you for your time."

Wurche's insides churned. She was not ready. She had to do something, come up with an idea to delay their going to Dagbon.

"Our problems started when we split into lines," she shouted. She couldn't stop her tongue. "If we came together as one people, one family, and solved problems *together*, imagine what that would be like. When we get to Dagbon, our strategy should be to get the other lines to work with us."

The room grew quiet. Etuto stood, dismissed everyone, and was about to head into his inner chamber when he turned and strode to Sulemana, Dramani and Wurche. Wurche's heart felt as if it had doubled in size and would burst out of her body. Mma walked over, her brow stitched in disapproval.

"Etuto, I apologize," said Wurche. "I had to speak—"

"You've heard the news yourself. You and Prince Adnan are to be married as soon as possible," Etuto said. Mma swallowed whatever she'd had to say, the frown replaced with pity. Pity was worse than anger.

"Etuto, I am entering this marriage for you," Wurche said. "Involve me in the negotiations in Dagbon. Please. Let's call the other lines and have Dagbon mediate."

Etuto nodded slowly and seemed to look through Wurche. She wasn't sure if he had heard her. He went back towards his inner chamber.

The next two hours were spent clearing out and closing up the huts on the farm. Donkey carts were loaded with people, baskets of food and provisions, and behind them ambled sheep and goats and people who were too heavy to sit on the carts. Ahead of the donkey carts, Etuto and a small army sat astride their horses, waiting for the mallam to give them their go-ahead. Etuto was in full military gear, his smock covered from head to toe in strings of square, brown leather talismans, two guns slung from his shoulder.

Mma sat behind Wurche on Baki—Etuto's idea. Neither of them was happy with the arrangement: Mma complained that Wurche rode her horse too fast, and the last person Wurche wanted to be with was someone who thought marriage was what she needed. Dramani had been instructed to ride at Wurche's side to keep them safe, which only increased her ire.

"We can take care of ourselves," Wurche said to Sulemana, also draped in a curtain of talismans. "You should have more faith in me."

"You're to be someone's wife," said Sulemana, too seriously. "We can't have anything happen to you."

"He's right," said Mma. "Wurche, calm down. These Dagbon men ... they won't let you get away with the things Etuto lets you off with. Their culture is very different from ours."

Sulemana was given a signal from the front and trotted off.

"You know that story you've told over and over?" Wurche said.

"Which one? I'm sure I haven't told anything over and over," said Mma.

"The Gonja story," said Dramani.

"Yes," said Wurche. "The one where the king tells his two sons, Umar and Namba, to go down to Bigu, the land of gold, to capture it and make it a part of his kingdom. The princes are brave and they subdue the people of Bigu, but Namba is told there is another land to conquer, leaves his brother and goes off with his soldiers to the east. He defeats the local people and settles in what is now Gonjaland. But that is the problem."

"It was a prophecy," said Mma. "Namba was told he would never be king in his own land."

"Yes, that *is* it. It's because everyone wants to be king. Even me. The moment Namba split away, it caused division. When Namba died, he left behind several lines. We don't think of ourselves as one people. We think of ourselves as Kanyase or Lepo or Singbung. If we don't stop, we're going to keep being fractured."

"But we've always done things this way. And people moved because they wanted to make sure there was enough land for everyone."

Wurche knew there was no getting through to her grandmother, so she said nothing else. Mma pinched Wurche's waist, as if to reassure her, but the gesture irked her.

"I'm sure you're worried about the wedding," Mma said, whispering so Dramani wouldn't hear. "What sunguru wouldn't be? When we get to Dagbon, the woman there will take you into a room and tell you things about your husband. Please listen to them. I am glad I convinced Etuto that you needed to learn Dagbani from a young age. Now, they won't be able to keep secrets from you."

Wurche grimaced at Mma's allusion to her virginity. *Sunguru.* Young, unmarried girl. When Wurche was about twelve, Mma bought a woman from Salaga to do the housework. The woman had a daughter called Fatima, the same age as Wurche. Wurche and Fatima grew inseparable. One afternoon, they sat in the small forest by Kpembe, and after Wurche had concluded one of her earnest speeches to get Etuto to include her in his close circle, she collapsed in joy by Fatima's side. She'd never forgotten the rush of accomplishment and love and promise she'd felt. Fatima's applause had said it all. It was an excellent speech, on why women made good leaders. Jaji had just taught her about Aminah of Zazzau. She hugged Fatima and they held on to each other for a long time until their embrace grew bolder. Wurche felt a strong need for more, an urge to surrender to a hunger her body had suddenly developed. And so their bodies met and searched and grinded as if hoping to unlock something hidden, something primal. And when Wurche found the pleasurable pearl at the base of her belly, she couldn't stop. She and Fatima searched each other's bodies every chance they got. Until the day Mma caught them. Fatima and her mother were sent away and Mma hadn't said a word about the incident since. Wurche was sure that Mma's obsession with marrying her off had begun that day.

"As I said, their customs are different from ours," continued Mma. "If you were marrying a Gonja man, you'd be locked up for seven days. But I don't know how it's done in Dagbon. On the wedding night, please cry. Cry when you're being paraded around. Cry when they present your husband to you. You're too proud to cry. But I also know you are reluctant to be married. You just have to show it."

Sulemana galloped back.

"We're splitting up," he said. "Etuto and the soldiers will take another way so they arrive in Dagbon faster. We'll go the usual route."

The usual route was twelve hours of traveling, and when they arrived in Dagbon, they met a crowd of drummers, women ululating "Wuliwuliwuliwuli!" and children weaving between their horses and donkeys. The palaces there were whitewashed, like in Kpembe, but larger. Mma said even though she'd been to Dagbon several times, she couldn't get over how much grander it was than Kpembe. Wurche herself had been a few times. It was grand, but she would much rather be in Salaga, which held people from all over the world. Dagbon was just a bigger Kpembe: full of pompous royals.

"Our wife is here! Our wife is here," sang the old women at the entrance.

A group of girls approached Baki and helped Mma and Wurche off. They led Wurche as if she were a delicate flower, into a large room where three older women sat on plush cushions before a tray of kola on a mat. Mma sat by Wurche and hooked her arm around hers. The older women watched Wurche gravely, until another set of women came in and sat behind her, enclosing her and Mma. Wurche should have run away. She was stupid to try to bargain with Etuto and now it was too late.

"We have to fatten her," said one of the old women.

"Yes, or he'll crush her," said a second.

They continued watching her and Wurche, tired of being treated like a doll, said, "When is the wedding?" Mma pretended to pick something from Wurche's dress and pinched her.

"Ah," said the first old woman, "impatient."

"Just impatient to get married to your son," said Mma.

"Well, we're still setting the date," said the second old woman, crunching into a chunk of kola. She sent the bowl around. "Let's get you clean for dinner. After that, we'll begin your lessons."

The mallams of Dagbon set the wedding for the day of the full moon, two weeks after Wurche's family arrived. The elite of Dagbon assembled to celebrate the union of their son with the daughter of Gonja. Cows, sheep and goats were slaughtered; new clothes were woven; drums were beaten from twilight to morning. And Etuto seemed the happiest man alive. He didn't look like a man about to fight for his life. He drank, ate one bite of meat after another, and had acquired a girl, not much older than Wurche, who kept supplying him with drinks. Wurche's gaze flitted from her father to her husband-to-be. Adnan was a man who didn't break rules, the old Dagbon ladies had told her. He would be a good family man. Loyal. A traditionalist. She watched him refuse calabashes of alcohol but accept well-wishers warmly, the flesh of his cheeks rising in orbs to smile at the people who greeted him. He was pleasant enough, handsome, some might even say. But, she couldn't imagine sharing her bed with him.

Wurche couldn't eat, and everyone was soused with millet beer or too full to notice. Drummers pounced on their drums with increased momentum. One of them played with such skill he appeared to be wristless. His hand slapped the skin of his drum with the speed of a sunbird's wings and he saw her looking. He approached her and rapped at the drum with everything he had. And she watched, entranced, almost forgetting where she was until she was seized from behind and dragged out of the circle of revelers. She was so startled she screamed and then, realizing what was happening, burst into tears. Mma would be pleased. She thrashed her arms and lashed at the person carrying her. She scratched the skin of the arm clamping her, and the person hit her hand and flipped her. The floor became ceiling and she saw the confused, cracked, bare feet of the people in the crowd. Some of the feet lifted up and down in tune with the drumming, others shuffled about with no rhythm, but when the feet grew purposeful, all pointing in the same direction, she knew it was over. She was carried into an incense-filled room and dropped onto the bed. Adnan sat across from her in light cotton trousers. The old ladies left the room and drew the curtain across the doorway.

Wurche tried to calm down, thinking it could be pleasurable, that what the old ladies had said about pain wouldn't apply to her. With Fatima, she'd learned of the places one had to pulse to get her heart racing. The old ladies had said to her, young men know where to put their hoses—any and everywhere. Steer him, make sure you are adequately prepared to receive him. A man like Adnan will not help, he will not take his time, he will not get you to your happy place before thinking of his pleasure. So prepare. And preparation begins in your mind. The imagination is a strong tool.

So that night she summoned two spirits: Moro's and Fatima's. His lean dark body, her gentle yet eager fingers. That had to be adequate preparation. She splayed her legs on the white linen sheet, toes curling and flexing. And he didn't wait. He pounced on her and ended her girlhood with such force she had to bite her tongue to clamp down the scream that would have escaped. It was excruciating. Moro and Fatima were long gone. She had become a pounding board. But then his face crumpled in worry; the expression seemed to ask if he should stop. Wurche encouraged him to go on. The old ladies had said to get the man to his happy place.

When he stiffened above her and grunted, all she wanted was to hide in a forest. He walked out of the room. No tenderness. And not a minute had gone by before the old ladies barged in, yanking the white sheet under Wurche. Her badge of honor, proudly showing: a splotch of red.

"Wuliwuliwuliwuli," sang the old ladies.

Aminah

They walked and walked. The horsemen raided villages and led their captives to an unknown destination and, as their numbers grew, bound them around trees in rings like obscene jewelry. The horsemen stole cattle, sheep and goats, and mixed up their captives so they wouldn't plot escapes. Aminah had managed to hold on to Hassana and Issa, whose skin clung to his bones, but they had lost Husseina. The horsemen had pried her from Hassana's grip and tied her to another group of people. Every chance she got, Hassana craned forward till she could see her twin, and only then would she relax. Children and women were tied neck to neck, their hands free. The wrists of the men—there weren't many of them—were bound with cord, and the strongest were restrained with wooden choke holds. Once, when a horseman was retying the cord around Hassana's neck, she choked. Her skin almost turned purple, and only then did the horseman relent. Husseina had stuck her head out and didn't break her gaze until the person behind her tripped over her.

A man tried to run away. Aminah didn't see the horsemen hang him, but in the bright morning light his slack body swayed from a tree, his feet dangling above the muddy soil. His hairless head, shaped like a cone of shea butter, rested against his right shoulder, his bare body gashed with lines of blood. The horsemen chatted around a fire. The smell of roasted meat wafted the way of the captives, digging into the emptiness in their bellies, into their nausea.

"I hope they have nightmares," Hassana shouted. With sunken eyes, she leered at the horsemen.

"It's okay," said Aminah, trying to hush her. "It will get better."

Hassana stopped talking but her eyes were fixed on the dead man. Aminah didn't think it was going to get better. She knew nothing, really. And she was wracked with guilt at possibly having enabled her mother's death. She should have gone into Na's hut to wake her up.

One woman—also Gurma like Aminah's people, but not from Botu—had said they were being sent to a lake with no beginning and no end. An infinite lake. She called it "big water." Her weaver husband had gone south to sell in the markets and had seen these pitiful people chained to the fronts of houses. He was told they would be put in boats controlled by white men and sent on the infinite lake. Her husband was shaken by the whole thing; he stopped asking questions. The woman had gone to visit her mother when the raiders attacked her mother's village. When they started tying her up, she knew her fate.

At least she'd had some preparation. For the rest of the captives, it was like walking in the forest on a night with no moon. They groped, bumped into things. Wild animals lurked and, sometimes, the animals bit.

A gust of wind sent the lifeless body swinging and wafted the smell of meat in Aminah's direction. A lump pressed hard against her sternum, from inside her body. The muscles of her belly contracted and convulsed. Up came bitter liquid. She swallowed it, suppressed it. It was horrible. She'd never had to swallow vomit before.

After the horsemen feasted, they poured water to quench their fire. They gave their porters the leftovers, and the porters gave some of their captured the bones and gristle. Issa didn't eat the tiny morsel of meat Aminah gave him.

Then the horsemen split into two groups. A porter ran along the file, counted up to a point and cut the cord. The group ahead of Aminah, Issa, and Hassana went to the left. That group included Husseina. They walked until the tall grass swallowed them. Where were they going? Would the two groups reunite? Aminah wanted to chase after them to get Husseina back, and just as she thought this, a shriek cut all the noises around to silence. It came from Hassana. Her scream froze blood. She doubled over, folded her arms over her belly, and wouldn't stop. A horseman trotted over and yelled something at her. She was now curling into a ball on the ground, her nails digging into the red soil. The horseman dismounted and walloped her with his riding whip. She didn't stop screaming. He kicked her ribs, but still she screamed. Only when a patch of red stained her dress, did Aminah break out of her trance. She fell to the ground and wrapped her little sister with her body and tried to stop the shrill scream by covering her mouth. The man's riding whip whacked Aminah's body until Hassana quieted down.

Hassana whimpered all afternoon. Aminah had lied; it wasn't getting better.

The captives tried to function as one. They urinated and emptied their bowels at the same time, under watchful eyes. When they were given food, they made sure everyone got at least a small piece. But it was impossible to stay united in such conditions. Some of them were in more pain than others. Issa struggled to walk, slowing down everyone behind him.

Aminah begged one of the porters to let her carry him even though she herself had very little strength. He now weighed next to nothing.

After walking for what must have been a week, like they were never going to stop, they arrived at a place unlike any other they had crossed. Rocks jutted up from the ground and trees grew everywhere. Okra-green grass carpeted the land, and even in her despair, Aminah found the green fresh and beautiful, the rocks mesmerizing. Not far off, vultures flew in circles. The horsemen dismounted, trussed up their stolen sheep and goats, and led the captives towards clusters of large rocks and trees with gnarly crowns. On a large boulder, people were gathered, eating. Aminah's heart pinched itself in what must have been excitement—the first time in a long time she had felt any hope. Perhaps that was the group that had left first. They could be reunited with Husseina after all. Aminah watched Hassana, but said nothing. Her reddened eyes stared ahead, focused on nothing in particular, as if she were sleepwalking. If they died, would they become spirit walkers? She had to stop herself from thinking like that. She pressed Hassana's hand—to transmit that something good might be on its way, but also to convince herself.

Up on the boulder, Aminah searched for faces from Botu. The group was unfamiliar. Suddenly, their captors whipped them and shouted at them to move. Aminah didn't understand the language, but the word "Babatu" was repeated. It was a name she'd heard in Botu, a man who was feared by the people of the caravans. If these ruthless horsemen were also afraid of him, he had to be a terrifying person. As that group left, any hope she had harbored dwindled.

Their horsemen led them to a patch of bald rock and one of them approached three women sitting behind large pots. Aminah couldn't see what was in them, but she had sat behind enough pots to know the thick, gurgling sound of boiling porridge. The horseman returned and, with his accomplices, divided the captives into smaller groups and sat them before oval troughs smeared with the muddy dregs of the previous group's leftover porridge. The women slopped the thick porridge into the troughs and the hollows steamed. Aminah cupped her hand to scoop the scalding gruel, blew on it, and led it to Issa's lips. He shook his head and pinched his lips shut tight. No matter how much she begged him, he wouldn't eat. The sight of the skin puckering above his lips began to annoy her. She felt a strong urge to slap him. Hassana swallowed a handful of porridge and twisted her face but kept eating. Finally, Aminah ate what Issa rejected. The millet porridge was sour, with no sweetness. After eating, they were led to larger holes, where water had collected, and from that they quenched their thirst. For the first time, Aminah's mind and body had pause. Something about having a full stomach calmed her. She thought of Baba and Na, wondering what had become of them. She had left things incomplete with her mother. And then she hadn't called her out of the room. How would she ever right that?

When the horsemen said it was time to go, Aminah got up, feeling full. Not satisfied, like after a good meal, but her body had more energy to keep going. Then down the hill they went. Below them spread groves of trees nestled in lush green grass. It was never this green in Botu, where Aminah wished she could return, and strangely, the sentiment of loss and nostalgia made her hope the big water would come soon. She didn't know what future it held, but she just wanted to stop walking.

Issa fell. He didn't trip or stumble. His body was sucked down, as if called by the earth. His skeletal form stacked itself against the gray metallic sheen of the rock. Aminah stared at the way his bony legs had crisscrossed, as if someone had delicately arranged him into a neat pile. It was Hassana who got down and tried to revive him. When they realized Aminah and Hassana were stalling, a horseman and porter raced over, shouting. As they drew closer, they saw what had happened. The horseman muttered and dismounted. He peeled Hassana off Issa and picked him up as if he were a bird. They carried him, then flung him over the rock. Above the rock, the circling vultures. Vultures were attracted to death. Aminah imagined below them was a cemetery of people like Issa who hadn't found the strength to go on. She pictured skeletons stacked on skeletons or flesh on skeletons, in Issa's case. Suddenly cold and afraid, she took Hassana's hand, small and dry, and tried to think of something to say to comfort her sister, but more to comfort herself. She felt the heaviness of her tongue. She swallowed several times, before words could come out.

"Maybe this is better for him," she said. "He was so weak."

"I hope he comes back as spirit walker to haunt these people," said Hassana, snatching her hand away to wipe her face, wet with tears.

When they left the rocky place, dying began to seem an attractive option. Running away was too costly; Aminah was so disoriented she didn't know which way home was, and she could fall into a worse situation. The name Babatu was frightening, if even these horsemen were afraid. And how would she do it?

Die? Swallow a poisonous bark? But she looked at Hassana and blocked her thoughts. They needed each other.

They arrived at a body of water, wide and unending. A gull flew down, settled on its glassy surface and glided away within minutes. Was this the big water? A porter waded ahead with a long stick and a horseman followed. The water reached the porter's shins, and the more he walked, poking the water with the stick, the higher it rose. When the water was level with his chest he waved at the horseman and changed direction. There, the water reached his neck, so he went back to his original path. She watched with wonder and anxiety; presumably they would have to do as the porter did.

The horseman beckoned everyone over. Some immediately splashed into the water while others tarried, and this caused a wave of confusion. Hassana and Aminah were pulled into the water. A girl panicked. She would only be shin-deep if she stood. She floundered and kicked and swallowed water. A horseman cantered over and whacked at them all, until even the struggling girl stood up. A foolish grin spread on her face when she realized the water was still shallow. The man next to her held her right hand, Hassana took her left, and they waded deeper. The girl grew agitated again towards the middle, where the water was as high as their necks. She went under, dragging Hassana down with her, and came up gasping as she pushed Hassana down. The girl was sucked down again, but Hassana still hadn't come up. The man and Aminah hauled them up and unwrapped the girl from Hassana, who wriggled free and desperately gulped air. When she recovered, she smacked the girl's face. The man pulled the girl away, and Aminah grabbed Hassana. For the rest of the crossing, the man carried the girl.

The water eventually came to an end. From what they had heard earlier, the big water had no beginning and no end. And they would be put on a big boat. It was not the big water. Crossing had exhausted Aminah. She wanted to yell at the horsemen, ask them why. She walked but she felt as if she wasn't in her body anymore. She wanted the earth to call her as it had called Issa, because she was tired, because she couldn't do it alone.

They arrived at a forest of trees with trunks like paths to a sky covered by thick leaves. They heard rustles, whistles, chirps, ribbits, trills, clucks and barks. The noises grew louder, as if the forest's animals were closing in on them. Aminah was relieved when the forest opened up into a clearing with several rectangular huts. Women washing clothes in a small stream didn't glance up at them. Some children came forward and ran alongside the human chain until they grew tired. Because they had arrived in broad daylight, Aminah knew these people would be spared. The people they met in the daytime always helped the horsemen.

They were funneled through a narrow path between two homes that opened up to a square, where five wide but short trees stood almost in a straight line. They were untied and led to three trees. The other two held other captives, but no Husseina. All but two horsemen went away. The woman who had mentioned the big water was tied to the same tree as Hassana and Aminah. They were in the shade, until the sun moved high in the sky and beat down on them like the anger Otienu would unleash if a woman offered him a sacrifice. Just as suddenly, rain clouds gathered and burst open on them, before disappearing as fast as they came. What was this place?

What had they all done to be punished like this? That was the only reason Aminah could think of for their troubles. That each of them had wronged someone. But what about poor Issa, who never hurt any living thing? Why did he die? Was dying a way of sparing him? Was dying better than living as they were? This was not a life. Not a destiny.

The weather cooled, the sun began its descent, and the square filled up. Men came in and out of the huts that lined the square and studied the new arrivals tied to the trees. They whispered to the horsemen.

That afternoon, several of the captives were unshackled and went with some of the men who had come out of the huts earlier. They never came back. Aminah told Hassana to hold her hand and not let go.

Evening fell. Hassana and Aminah relaxed their grip when no one else came. Mosquitoes feasted on them. Two women brought them leaves with some kind of sweet yellow tuo and stew, and that meal tasted like the best thing Aminah had ever eaten.

"Ah!" exclaimed the big-water woman. Aminah almost jumped out of her skin, thinking some animal had climbed onto her neighbor's body.

"I'm bleeding. I usually know when it will start, but these people have affected my timing, everything."

She cupped her fingers and then dug her nails into the soil near the tree's exposed root. When the hole was as wide as her palm and deep enough to fit her whole hand, she sat over it and lifted her wrapper. Aminah hoped her own blood would stay inside her, for as long as it needed to. She didn't want to be walking around with blood running down her legs.

That night, she slept better than she had in a long time.

"I didn't sleep," said Hassana the next day. "I heard animals howling and creeping closer." She'd pictured the animals coming to maul everyone as they slept, and had kept watch.

A short man with a white-and-black cloth thrown over his left shoulder came with one of the horsemen. The horseman whipped Aminah, ordering her to stand. She grabbed Hassana's hand and the two of them scrambled up. The men studied them and said something to the horseman. They left and went to the other trees. The short man returned. He came and went three times, and Aminah could see the horseman shuffling his feet back and forth, losing patience. Hassana clawed Aminah's palms, and Aminah prayed and prayed to Otienu.

"These two," said the short man in Hausa, pointing to Hassana and Aminah.

The horseman patted the man on the back and they went into one of the houses on the square. Eventually, Hassana and Aminah were untied from the tree and led away by the short man. Aminah wished, then, that she were Husseina, able to share dreams with Hassana to hatch a plan to escape.

A donkey and cart were tied to a tree.

"Get on," said the man. "Not far from here."

Aminah climbed up and then helped Hassana. They sat on a jute sack, next to a white ewe and the forest closed in on them as they rode away.

Wurche

A week after she was married, her father and his soldiers, backed by the Dagbon army, galloped to Salaga-Kpembe to declare war. Wurche was not allowed to leave the compound, not with her father's enemies at large. The old women of Dagbon, who were trying to plump her up in preparation for childbearing, were adamant about keeping her cloistered. She swallowed the large chunks of beef without telling them that her body never put on weight. A week after the war started, a messenger was sent to summon Mma, Wurche and the rest of the family back to Kpembe. Wurche was glad to be out in the open and back on her horse, but what she saw in Salaga saddened her. Houses had crumbled to ash. Walls were pocked with bullet holes. The soup that was Salaga was reduced to bones and char. Etuto had won the war, but the prize they'd been fighting for had lost its shine.

"Wo yo!" said Mma behind Wurche.

Wurche kicked her shins against Baki's flank and the horse shot off. Mma shrieked and grabbed Wurche's waist. They flew by the main Salaga market, the Lampour mosque, the smaller market, her teacher Jaji's quarters, and galloped up the road to Kpembe. All the months of doing nothing, of being bullied and force-fed, were crystallized into the rush of fear washing over her.

Mma's crossed arms pressed into Wurche's belly as she screamed that Wurche had lost her mind.

When they got to the top of the hill, fifteen minutes later, Wurche's fears were not assuaged. The palace was, surprisingly, still whole, but its people were not. Several men loitered about the courtyard, some of them limping, others cleaning their guns. Two men were examining an arrow sticking out of another man's shoulder. Only when she saw her brothers did she calm down. She reined Baki in and Mma scrambled down. The old lady bent over, gasping, holding her chest as if she were about to keel over and die. Dramani rushed to her, and she grabbed his face to make sure he was real. Then she pressed him to her chest. Wurche went to Sulemana, who hadn't picked himself up to greet them. His face was contorted in pain. His leg, raised on a pouf, was gashed open. She touched the skin around the wound.

"Gun, knife or arrow?" she asked. Sulemana winced and brushed her hand aside.

"Arrow."

"Where is Etuto?" she asked, fearing the worst.

"Celebrating," said Dramani.

"Wo yo," said Mma now seeing Sulemana. The old lady burst into tears and wrapped her flesh around Sulemana's head.

Wurche asked why no one had taken care of Sulemana's wound and he said Etuto had poured rum on it, that there were other people with worse injuries who had to be seen to. She rushed out of the palace, searching the dry grass for signs of life. Mma had showed her useful plants for curing wounds, but the dry season had already sapped life out of the bush and the war had only worsened things. She found nothing. When she went back, Mma was still in tears, clutching Sulemana, looking around at the soldiers. It was only when Wurche said he could lose his leg that the old lady let him go. She headed to her room and Wurche followed.

"A room needs to breathe or it dies," said Mma as Wurche sneezed through the dust. "I can't believe we've caused another senseless war."

She picked up a pot filled with little bundles of herbs and a large gecko scuttled out of the way. She ransacked the pot and grunted when she found a packet wrapped in indigo. She handed a strip of cotton to Wurche and they walked back outside. Pressing the herbs together with a splash of water from the well in the courtyard, she lifted Sulemana's leg and he grimaced as she set it on her thighs. When she began pressing the poultice to the gash, Sulemana poured out a scream so raw it silenced everyone in the compound. Etuto rushed out of his room. Adnan followed; Wurche had almost forgotten about him.

"My family!" slurred Etuto, making his way towards them. Wurche, tasked with tying the cloth around the wound, tried to dodge his rum-laced embrace, but he overpowered her. She gave in to his hug.

"You, my daughter, are the reason I am alive." He patted her back. His eyes were sunken, drained of joy, even though he was smiling. "I won't forget that."

He went back to his room. She turned to face her husband. He'd come out of *her* room. She wondered if her brothers had assigned it to him or if he'd gone looking for it himself. She didn't know him at all. She couldn't anticipate the kinds of decisions he'd make. She hadn't made the effort to find out who he was behind his mask, but something told her he was a man intent on never taking off the mask. She bent her knees ever so slightly, as a sign of respect, and went back to bandaging Sulemana's wound.

That evening, the whole family gathered in three circles around bowls of tuo and groundnut soup. Wurche pressed for details of the war. Adnan sat in her circle, next to her. She wondered if she would ever grow used to the idea of having a husband with whom she had to do everything.

"We camped for a night just outside Salaga to do the Gangang dance," Dramani said. "We looked like fools, but if Nafu and his men came upon us, we'd still be awake. The morning of the battle we wore leather pouches with holy inscriptions that Etuto's mallam had supplied, and charms we soaked in millet beer and gin. We lined our eyes with kohl and polished our boots."

"Why kohl? To prevent dust from getting in your eyes?"

"It's a ritual. We do it to feel confident. Nobody wants to break rituals because it can lead to defeat," Dramani explained. "Our boots were impressive. Then we lined up. Etuto prepared his rifle-musket. Suddenly, he stood up, thrust the rifle into the air and shouted, 'If we call death "mother," we will die! If we call death "father," we will die! Let us call death by its own name and let it do its worst.' Then he took a huge swig from his gourd, and passed it on. I took a large gulp. It was horrible."

"Why? What was it?" asked Wurche. She had to admit that Dramani told a good story. He would probably be a better student for Jaji. Storytelling, Jaji said, was the best way to teach lessons.

"It was a soup of ground monitor lizard mixed with bitter herbs Etuto's mallam gave him. I swallowed it, wiped my mouth, slung my quiver over my back, mounted my horse and followed Etuto. He had charged forward. We stood opposite a cavalcade of men from our Kanyase line who were allied with the other two lines. Our own uncles. Imagine! At first they seemed intimidating, assembled on their horses, but when I looked behind us and saw Adnan and the Dagbon army bolstering our numbers, I felt confident. I faced the enemy and saw familiar faces: Nafu, Shaibu ... Sulemana's friends. Our friends, really. And yet there we were. Etuto inched towards Nafu's army. It was their one last chance to talk, but an arrow shot through the air and landed just in front of his horse, making his horse balk.

"Etuto raised his gun and pointed it at the enemy camp. He fired into the air and a cloud of smoke burst forth. I charged forward. Etuto and Sulemana and a line of Gonja soldiers were ahead, waving their rifles in the air before they let out a round of shooting. After shooting, they drew back and were replaced by a line of Dagbon men. Etuto and his men reloaded their rifles. I took an arrow from my quiver. After the Dagbon soldiers fired their shots, we stepped forward and replaced them."

"Did anyone die?"

"Many people. A man by me went down. A bullet ripped through his neck leaving behind a gaping hole that spat blood as he slunk off his horse. The sun woke up and at this point we were in the Salaga market. Nafu's men must have realized that they were losing, so they set fire to as many buildings as they could. I am told their followers are still burning houses in Salaga."

"There is nothing left to burn in Salaga. The town is burnt. What happened next?"

"We moved like lightning. More people were knocked off their horses. An arrow grazed my shoulder, but didn't pierce my skin.

"Sulemana waved his rifle in the air and as he did so, an arrow tore through his leg. He stopped his gun show, cocked the rifle's butt over his shoulder, and shot and killed his assailant before drawing back. Every time I moved ahead, my horse stumbled over bodies sprawled on Salaga's red soil. By the time we got to the other end of the market, Nafu's soldiers had retreated. Etuto, Sulemana, Adnan and the Dagbon soldiers shot their guns into the air. We'd won."

"Wo yo," said Wurche, watching Mma go from circle to circle, adding meat to the groundnut soup.

"Praise be to Allah, we survived," said Sulemana, reaching for a chunk of meat.

"Why is Etuto the only one celebrating?" said Wurche. "I don't understand. Why aren't you all celebrating? You don't know how many times I almost got on Baki to come and fight with you."

"My aunts would never have let that happen," Adnan said, patting Wurche's thigh. "But if we were in Dagbon, my dear, master drummers would be singing all our praises by now. You've seen how we do things there."

"These were people we knew," Dramani responded; a relief to Wurche, who was about to be rude. She had to appear grateful since Etuto's victory was, in large part, thanks to Adnan and his army. "People we went to the mosque with ... It was a costly battle. I've thought a lot about what you've been saying, Wurche. We're more divided than ever."

Wurche, encouraged, said, "Yes, Dagbon and Gonja do things differently. We don't even speak the same language.

And in the search to expand both our territories, we've gone to war with each other. But, see, we came together and Etuto won the war. If we *all* come together, we can unite the north."

"You Gonja men are too sentimental," said Adnan. *Men.* He'd dismissed her.

"No, Dramani is right," said Sulemana. "These were our brothers we fought, not some enemy from a strange land. There's nothing sentimental about that."

Adnan seemed to sulk, so Sulemana tried to placate him. "The truth is if we hadn't had Adnan and Dagbon with us, we wouldn't have stood a chance. We don't know if Nafu's still alive. Some people say he's dead. Some say he turned into a crocodile and is now in a river somewhere."

"I've concluded that war is senseless," said Dramani. "I'm going to ask Etuto for permission to move to the farm after this."

Wurche raised her brows. Apart from farming, how else would Dramani occupy his time? Farming was for people from slave villages like Sisipe. She wondered how Etuto would react.

"And Shaibu?" said Wurche.

"In Kete-Krachi," said Sulemana. "He retreated faster than an antelope escaping a lion. I didn't see him fight at all. Kete-Krachi is where most of them are. Etuto wants to go after them, but we need to recover first."

"Why Kete-Krachi?" asked Wurche.

"To forge an alliance with the Germans based there, since Etuto collaborated with Dagbon and seems aligned with the British," said Dramani, "I suppose the only big allies left are the Asante or the Germans. Going with the Asante would be servitude all over again, so they chose the Germans."

"But, Etuto is still negotiating things with the British," said Wurche. "He hasn't formally aligned with them."

"Sides are being taken," said Dramani. "And I have a feeling it's only going to get worse."

Three days after Wurche's arrival, those who had not fled to Kete-Krachi gathered in Etuto's palace with representatives of the paramount chief of Gonja, the Yagbumwura, the kingmaker. Etuto rode a tall new horse, freshly imported from Mossi, with meaty shoulders and forelegs and a shiny brown coat. Wurche longed to take it for a ride.

Etuto dismounted. The Yagbumwura's spokesperson put a new striped smock on him and gravely spread an old lion skin and an equally worn leopard skin on the soil. The skins of founding father Namba. He signaled for Etuto to come forth, and as he sat on the skins, one of the drummers pounded three times. No face smiled. A stranger might think it was a funeral. It should have been festive, but half of the people who should have been there had fled or died. Wurche was glad she had given Etuto reason to celebrate at the wedding. After the mallams left, people in Salaga-Kpembe came to greet Etuto, bringing gifts of sheep, cloth, gold, myrrh and slaves. Food and millet beer cheered the air somewhat, but the whole enskinning ceremony had been so sobering that Wurche spent the rest of the afternoon in Mma's room, which was where she went to avoid Adnan.

Wurche was convinced something was germinating in her, but she wasn't ready. She'd barely adjusted to the idea of living with someone else and couldn't begin to fathom having to take care of a baby. Every day she eyed Mma's pot of medicines, but the old lady lurked about her room as if she suspected Wurche's intentions. The longer Wurche left it, the harder it would become to purge herself of Adnan's child.

Early one morning, she rode Baki into Salaga. The air still stank of smoke, the narrow streets were filled with rubble and rubbish. "What did we do here?" she whispered. By marrying Adnan, she was complicit in this damage. If Etuto hadn't had the support of the Dagbon army, he'd never have declared war. But he might also be dead.

The smell of rotten eggs wafted from the wells, odorous from sitting too long. The stench shot bile up Wurche's throat. She paused till the nausea passed. A lone drum was being beaten, noncommittal. The market square only held a handful of people, slowly rebuilding, picking up their lives, continuing where they left off. It was reassuring, the resilience of people.

Before she arrived in the smaller market, where potions, herbs and purgatives were sold, Wurche saw Moro. He was herding a group of captives. He disappeared behind a rectangular hut, left his slaves behind, walked into the hut. She got off Baki, tied her to a tree and plotted. She could enter the hut and pretend it was the wrong place. Or she could just wait for him and greet him. But he could be her father's enemy. Could she greet him in the street?

He came out and she panicked. She was in his path, but he was studying something in his hand and bumped into her.

"The beautiful one who frowns," he said, beaming.

"I can't be seen with you."

"Why?" His expression was softer than the day they met, when he'd beat Shaibu at the races and whacked the slave woman.

"You're in Shaibu's camp."

"I'm in nobody's camp."

"Can we talk somewhere privately?" As a Gonja princess, she could do whatever she wanted, but as a wife of Dagbon, she couldn't. It was better to avoid angering Dagbon, on whose support Etuto still depended.

He suggested the hut he'd just walked out of. Inside, two men sat across from each other on a mat. She curtsied quickly and followed him into a second chamber. It was dark, reeked of fermenting millet, and was probably teeming with rats.

"How come you're still in Salaga and not in Kete-Krachi?"

"I am working."

"How do I know you didn't fight against my father? Shaibu is your friend."

"I've known Shaibu for a long time and I work for him, but I didn't take part in this war."

His words pleased her. A pit formed in her stomach. The world between her legs lit up, so when he reached forward and touched her cheek gently, she pressed his hand against it. This was everything. She'd waited so long for this. She'd dreamed up all sorts of scenarios. But the reality of being with him was a thousand times better. His smell—a little sweaty and nutty—hadn't made its way into her fantasies. Nor the feel of his skin against hers—calloused but gentle. She knelt before him, and he seemed to hesitate, but said nothing as she took off her smock, then his. He never broke his gaze, even as she quietly, frantically, sat astride him, cupping his flesh into hers.

"Katcheji," said Moro, after. Yes, she'd strayed from her husband and was immoral, but that wasn't her first thought. Instead, she mulled over how different this was from being with Adnan, who often left her feeling like a hollow vessel. This time she was pleased. She was both satiated and hungry, as if her body would burst from fullness and pleasure and the only solution was more. "What am I doing with a married woman?" continued Moro. "And a princess of two powerful kingdoms, at that. It can mean serious trouble for me. Probably not for you. I often find myself doing things and wondering how I ended up there. Then I tell myself it's because I was raised to believe in destiny. I allow things to happen. It's a dangerous way to live."

She didn't want to talk. When she said nothing, he laid his head against her chest. In one of her lessons with her teacher, she learned that the adulterer develops a stink worse than carrion. For a fleeting second, it scared her. What *had* she done? She was an adulterer. And yet, claiming the title inexplicably banished her fear.

"This is not dangerous. No one will find out." She felt invincible. "Don't go. Let's spend our days in Salaga."

"For now, I have to come and go. I work in Kete-Krachi too. And you have a husband."

"When will you return?"

"If this is our destiny, soon. We can meet here. Maigida, the landlord, is a very discreet man."

On the ride back to Kpembe, she replayed images of what had just happened. Twice she stopped Baki and wondered if it had been a dream. Then she realized that she hadn't taken care of what was possibly sprouting inside her. She'd just complicated her situation.

That evening, when her monthly blood trickled down her legs, she rejoiced.

Aminah

A list of noisy things: lizards, dogs, donkeys, hyenas, chickens and guinea fowl, birds in general, flies and mosquitoes, geckos mating, Wofa Sarpong (the short man) during the day, Wofa Sarpong talking to his wives, Wofa Sarpong fighting with his wives, Wofa Sarpong's wives fighting with each other, Wofa Sarpong's wives pounding dried leaves or fufu, Hassana having her hair braided by Aminah, heavy rainfall on the thatch roof, the bracelets clinking up and down Wofa Sarpong's first wife's arms, the second wife's singing, the third wife's children yowling, local drummers coming around to beg, Wofa Sarpong fitting a cart on his donkey, big pigs, little pigs, the village crier bringing news from town, Aminah's stomach most days.

A list of quiet things: the sun, snakes, stars, Aminah's heart every morning, the thick forest surrounding Wofa Sarpong's farm, seeds, millet seedlings bursting from seeds, the furry mold sprouting on everything, Hassana since arriving on the farm, Wofa Sarpong entering Aminah and Hassana's room at night, his excited exhalations, Hassana breathing by Aminah, Wofa Sarpong slinking out, the night, heaviness falling and contouring every part of Aminah till morning came, Wofa Sarpong's wives on the goings-on in Aminah's room, moonlight.

He kept Aminah's virginity intact. She wondered why, but to ask may have invited him to go beyond forcing himself into her mouth. She wanted to hide Hassana from that shameful thing he was doing to her. The thing they were doing. She considered herself involved, because deep inside she knew that by sinking in her teeth, she could change her life and Hassana's. Even Wofa Sarpong must have known this fact— which was why he always appeared scared during the act. And yet, she couldn't bring herself to do anything but lie still as he clutched at her face and throat until he got excited. When he'd get up to leave, her legs would grow heavy, her heart sore. She was always too ashamed to move. She would lie there, a part of her, of all things, grateful. That he didn't take his act beyond her mouth meant if she ever got back to Botu, she wouldn't be a ruined woman.

Botu. Did it still exist? She wasn't even sure how far away they were, but this place was so different. Even the smell of rain wasn't the same; more saturated, suffocating. It was after Wofa Sarpong left Aminah that she often thought of her parents and of home. She wondered if Baba made Na do the act Wofa Sarpong was forcing on her. Would love make it any less belittling? She began, again, to convince herself that her parents had had a great love, despite what her last days in Botu had led her to believe. She decided that by leaving their rooms when the raiders came, she and her siblings let go of Baba. Issa-Na's going away was a betrayal of him. But not Na. She stayed in her hut because of her faith in Baba. It had to be her way of waiting for him. Sadness took over when she thought these things.

Quietness had seeped and settled into Hassana when they arrived on the farm, about ten months before. It spread within her like the mold that grew on their clothes, on their sheets, on everything. Whether it was because she realized there was no hope of returning to their old life, to her twin, or when Wofa Sarpong started skulking into their room, she didn't say.

"Your sister is strange," Sahada often remarked. She was a girl whose father owed Wofa Sarpong a debt and had pawned her to him until he could pay. Aminah wanted to ask Sahada to leave Hassana alone, but she merely grunted. Sahada must have thought Aminah strange, too, just a hair more approachable than Hassana. The only time glimpses of the old Hassana appeared were the moments when she sat between Aminah's knees to get her hair braided. Often, Aminah would intentionally over-tighten a braid and, forgetting herself, Hassana would scream and hit her sister's hand. Then just as quickly, she'd slide back into silence, relinquishing her head with quiet resignation.

Hassana washed the clothes and cooking pots of Wofa Sarpong and his family. The skin of her poor little hands became like land during the rainy season: ridged and eroded. Aminah worked on the farm, planting seeds, removing weeds, watering the seedlings, scaring away birds, harvesting millet and sorghum. She fed the pigs Wofa Sarpong kept in a thatch enclosure. She worked with four girls, three of whom had also been plucked from their villages at night. Sometimes, they went into the forest to forage for kola. It wasn't kola season and, according to the first wife, girls weren't supposed to harvest kola, but Wofa Sarpong was overeager and would insult them every time they returned empty-handed. On the farm, Wofa Sarpong's first wife and her sons supervised the girls, making sure they weren't plotting to escape or steal. She was the only person who spoke enough Hausa to communicate clearly with Hassana and Aminah.

In some ways, life wasn't that different from Aminah's routine in Botu. Some people had begun to remind her of people from home. Only now, she didn't laugh much. She didn't dream anymore. And she had a man forcing her to do bad things.

Wofa Sarpong was away often, with his donkey and cart. It was a mixed blessing when he was gone. His wives made the girls clean their rooms, Wofa Sarpong's room, their children's rooms, and after that they'd barely feed them. But Hassana and Aminah could relax at night without worrying that he was going to burst in. And, sometimes, the other girls would invite them to their room, separated from Aminah's by a wall of woven palm fronds.

"In Botu, we had a water hole and sometimes the boys would pretend to be crocodiles and hippopotami to scare us," Aminah told them once.

"In Larai," another girl said, "when it rained, it was such a special occasion. We all ran out to dance in the light rain. There was no lightning and thunder."

When they whispered these stories of home among themselves, Hassana barely spoke, but smiled when someone said something funny.

Wofa Sarpong's wives were small women with hair cropped close to their scalps. The first wife's face was carved with two sharp scars on either cheek. The second wife sang her words, which made Aminah think she would be sympathetic, but she was vile. The third wife sounded like a man. Aminah watched Wofa Sarpong argue with his women when they told him they'd run out of food; he would yell and rue the day he married them and sometimes he would let them go without provisions until they got on their knees and begged. It made her think of her parents' relationship. If they ever argued, it

was because her father had forgotten something. Head in the clouds, Na always said of him.

Days, weeks, months went on like that. Hassana said nothing. Aminah worked on the farm and allowed Wofa Sarpong to use her body to excite himself. On festive occasions they inherited clothes from the first wife.

Wofa Sarpong bought more girls to work on the farm and two girls moved into the room with Hassana and Aminah. It didn't stop him from coming in for his nightly visit.

There were days when the sameness of it all got to Aminah. She would cry and wonder what the point of staying alive was. But she would see Hassana sitting by her, her shoulders rising and falling with each breath, and chide herself for thinking only of her own happiness.

One morning, Hassana woke up drenched in sweat. She tapped Aminah and couldn't stop pouring out words.

"It was bright where I was," she began. "We were in a boat on a big lake surrounded by tiny hills and the water was two different kinds of blue. In front, the water was light blue like the sky and in the back it was a deep blue, a blue I hadn't seen before. There was a line between the blues. And then as we got off and stepped onto wet soil we saw that right next to the water was a thick forest. It looks like here but because of the lake it was brighter. The sun shone through. There were palm-like trees, but they were really tall. There were many of us getting off the boat. I couldn't see faces, but there was a lot of confusion. And that's where the dream ended.

"I've never seen a place like that before. Even the boat. It was big and had white squares of cloth on top of it that blew in the wind. It only means one thing. These are her dreams. Husseina is alive!"

The village crier came from town, yelled something and was off with the speed of a mouse. Sahada's family had settled nearby and she understood Twi, the Asante language, so at first Aminah would ask her to translate, but it was never anything interesting—a new provision from the coast, a new church opening up. So she'd stopped asking for help. Also, she'd started understanding snatches of Twi. That afternoon, the girls were taking a break after a sweltering and grueling day, and after the village crier left, Wofa Sarpong called and lined them up in order of height. His wives shuffled out of their rooms to watch. He pointed at Hassana.

"You Adwoa," he said in bad Hausa. Hassana looked confused. "You understand? You Adwoa."

He pointed at the next girl, said she was Abena. He was changing their names. The third girl's was Akua, Aminah's name was Yaa, and he went on like that, assigning names that corresponded with days of the week. Yaa. Thursday-born. Then he said their last name was to be Sarpong, his name. Yaa Sarpong. Aminah said it a few times in her head.

Wofa Sarpong said a lot in Twi and then turned to those who hadn't understood him. "Inspector coming. You behave fine, understand? You don't talk. You use the name I give you."

Aminah was surprised by the speed with which she'd picked up Twi. Sometimes the words were similar to hers, like "di," the word for eat. She could even eavesdrop on simple conversations between Wofa Sarpong and his wives. She learned that they lived near a town called Kintampo. And she learned that this Kintampo was within another place called the Gold Coast, which was governed by white men. But complex sentences were harder to understand, so when they went back to the abrofo nkatie tree under whose ample shade they had been lounging to keep cool, she asked Sahada to explain.

"People aren't allowed to buy, sell or own slaves here," said Sahada, picking up an abrofo nkatie fruit and biting greedily into its fleshy red pulp, its juices running down her wrist. "If the inspector finds out that Wofa Sarpong has slaves he'll be fined heavily. Of course, a lot of people still have slaves, but they pretend the slaves are their children."

"But me and Hassana look nothing like him," said Aminah. She pointed at the new girls. "And they are much, much taller than he is."

"All he has to do is act nice and give the inspector some gifts and he'll be fine. That's what my father does," said Sahada, slurping on what was left of the flesh of the fruit. She spat the fruit's woody leftovers onto her palm, then searched under the tree until she found a rock. Laying the seed on its side on top of the abrofo nkatie's exposed root, she whacked at the seed until it cracked. She sucked her teeth in annoyance as she split open the mushed nut.

Sahada started talking about how miserly Wofa Sarpong was because he bought slaves cheaply in Kintampo and sold them together with kola in Salaga for a lot of money. Aminah asked her where Salaga was, but she had no idea.

The inspector didn't come when he was expected. He finally showed up, one afternoon, when the girls were winnowing bowls of millet. Aminah heard Wofa Sarpong's voice grow squeaky as he squealed and chased after a man in a round hard hat, a light brown shirt, shorts and dusty feet. The man acted as if he'd been there before and knew his way around. It was the same kind of confidence she saw in some of the

Hausa traders who came with the caravans. It was the walk of someone who'd been given a small spoon of power and treated it as if it were a barrel. Wofa Sarpong's wives and children trooped out. Sahada translated for Aminah.

"He's saying he knows Wofa Sarpong has slaves," Sahada said. "Sarpong just said, 'But this *is* my family. What slaves?'" Wofa Sarpong took furtive glances at them. "He said the inspector should ask us himself."

Wofa Sarpong went to his first wife and asked her to mention her name and the names of her children. Next was the second wife and her brood. Then the third and her children. Then the inspector, who at first seemed uninterested in the whole naming ceremony, looked straight at the girls.

"My nieces, my children," said Wofa Sarpong. They weren't standing in order of height this time. Aminah went first, said her name was Yaa Sarpong. The other girls mentioned their new names.

"Hassana," said Hassana. She said it crisply and the silence that followed, although brief, could be sliced.

"Her late father was my brother," offered Wofa Sarpong. "He married a Northern woman. Very beautiful. You know how they are tall. She's Hassana Sarpong."

The inspector regarded her and called her forward.

"Where are you from?" he asked her.

"From Botu. I am the second daughter of Baba Yero and Aminah-Na."

Wofa Sarpong rattled a string of words and then said, pointing to his head, "She's not correct."

The inspector removed two cards from his front pocket and handed them to Wofa Sarpong. "You deserve five cards. This is your first warning. I'll be back."

"Yessir," groveled Wofa Sarpong.

As the inspector left the farm, Wofa Sarpong followed him, praying for him to be blessed with many children. Hassana's fingers were back in the bowl of millet, looking for stones that had to be removed. Aminah wanted to hide her.

When Wofa Sarpong beat his children, he *beat* them. You could hear the heavy thwacks as he raised his arms to the sky and landed his special whip on his children's flesh. He didn't stop until all the anger had drained out of him. Hassana and Aminah had been lucky so far. At most, they had been knocked on the head or screamed at to work harder, but they had never tasted Wofa Sarpong's lashes.

Loud footsteps approached. Wofa Sarpong was coming back. Hassana didn't react as she worked on her millet. His children squeezed out of their rooms, their faces cracked into wicked smiles of anticipation.

Hassana didn't look up at him, which must have angered him even more. He grabbed her ear and used that to lift her up from the ground. Her bowl of millet came crashing down and the tiny gray seeds spread on the red soil, forming the image of a fan, on which Aminah fixed her eyes as he whacked his cane against Hassana's body over and over. The spilled millet grew blurry. Hassana was screaming.

You should get up and protect her, Aminah kept thinking, but she was paralysed. *What is wrong with you? Do something!* She forced herself up and ran forward, sandwiching herself between Hassana and Wofa Sarpong. The silence that followed was thick and pregnant. He hesitated before unleashing the next lash. But before it landed on Aminah, Hassana shoved her sister out of the way so it hit her. Aminah watched motionless as Wofa Sarpong continued to whack Hassana. When he stopped, he was drenched in sweat, his cloth bunched at his feet. Gruffly, he pulled up the cloth, over his shorts, and returned to his room with his whip. Aminah dashed to Hassana, coiled on the ground, blood soaking through her wrapper. Sahada came over and the two girls carried Hassana to their room.

"Get leaves from the abrofo nkatie tree," said Sahada. Aminah rushed to the tree and broke off a thin branch with flat wide leaves. She was running back to the hut when Wofa Sarpong burst out of his room, trailed by his second wife.

"Yes, she needs to go," sang the woman.

"Bring her," he ordered. Aminah dropped the branch and she and Sahada carried Hassana out. "Put her there." He was pointing at the donkey cart.

"Please," Aminah started, trying to delay whatever was going to happen next.

"Fast, fast!" he barked.

"Please, take us together."

Wofa Sarpong glared at her with bulging, veined eyes. She stood with her arms at her sides as Sahada and Wofa Sarpong hoisted Hassana onto the back of the cart. Wofa Sarpong climbed up the cart, didn't say another word, and hit the donkey to get it moving. Sahada grabbed the branch Aminah had dropped and threw it at Hassana, telling her to chew the leaves to rub on her skin. Aminah ran alongside the cart till her chest was ready to explode, but Wofa Sarpong did not stop.

When she returned to her room, everything that happened sank in. Hassana had wanted to be beaten. Now that she'd connected with her Husseina, she wasn't going to stay on the farm. She did everything so Wofa Sarpong would get rid of her.

When Wofa Sarpong's donkey clip-clopped back a few hours later, Aminah rushed out, praying he'd had a change of heart, but Hassana had been traded for bales of cloth, a bag of salt, farm tools, and two chickens.

What is wrong with me? Aminah wondered. She wasn't in physical chains: there were days after working on the farm, when she would spend hours with no one monitoring her. The land beyond the farm was thick with forest, probably bursting with wild animals, but she was sure no one would come after her. And yet she stayed.

"She get good buyer in Kintampo," Wofa Sarpong said, later that evening, scrambling to his feet and covering himself. "He'll take her to the big water."

Wurche

A group of women, old and young, sat on mats outside Jaji's hut, in the shadow of the tall Lampour mosque with its slanting walls and spokes from roof to floor. Their eyes patiently watched Wurche, waiting for her to teach them Nana Asma'u's poem, "A Warning II." Wurche felt as if her heart had been pushed into her mouth and she was surprised and annoyed by her nerves. After all those times she'd practiced speeches to Fatima in the Kpembe forest, she thought she'd breeze through teaching Jaji's students, but now she didn't even know what to do with her hands. She clasped them behind her and pressed her fingers into her back. She watched as some of the women wiped their faces with their brightly colored scarves. She heard distant drums. She heard bells. She smelled and tasted the woodiness of a fire. The egg-like smell of Salaga's one hundred wells was carried over by the wind. Flies buzzed and zipped around her. Her senses seemed to have multiplied. The air was wet and heavy. She wiped her face and recited:

> Women, a warning.
> Leave not your homes without good reason.
> You may go out to get food or to seek education.
> In Islam, it is a religious duty to seek knowledge.
> Women may leave their homes freely for this.

Repent and behave like respectable married women.
You must obey your husbands' lawful demands.
You must dress modestly and be God-fearing.
Do not imperil yourselves and risk hell-fire.
Any woman who refuses, receives no benefit,
The merciful Lord will give her the reward of the damned.

"Good," said Jaji, standing opposite Wurche in her trademark woven hat. She pressed her fingers together under her chin and hunched her shoulders, the posture she assumed when she wanted to gently admonish. "Now, Wurche will repeat the verse again, slowly, so you can start memorizing the lines."

That morning, Wurche hadn't stopped to contemplate the poem, but as she recited the lines again, she realized how much the poem was a warning for her. She had left her home to pursue education, but the last thing she was doing was behaving like a respectable Muslim woman. She banished thoughts of ending up in the raging fires of hell and instead observed, with increased amusement, the women struggling to repeat the poem. By the time they'd gone through it a fifth time, Wurche felt her nerves disappear.

The lesson was over by midday. Jaji called Wurche a natural leader, and said with Wurche's help, she would be able to reach more women, a feat which would please the imam, who was convinced women could make sure their husbands stayed in the faith. He had been so unhappy since the war he was considering leaving Salaga. A place without a spiritual leader was doomed. And as Jaji prattled on about how difficult life had become since the war, Wurche panicked. This was now the only reason Adnan let her out of the house—to teach these women. Her panic was imbued with a sense of loss—an absence of something she couldn't even name—and another sentiment: that of being covered by a thick cloth, a feeling that grew worse when Jaji asked her how her husband was, a feeling that stayed with her when she went to the rectangular hut (where she and Moro had done katcheji) and found it locked. It grew especially heavy when she went home and sat wordlessly by her husband during the evening meal.

The heaviness that had cloaked her lifted when she rode Baki and spent time with Moro. Once, riding down to Jaji's, she crossed paths with him as he led a sluggish queue of men and women chained to each other, followed by two others on horseback. Moro moved with solemn purpose, and when he noticed her waving, he smiled, signaled to the other horsemen, and rode to her.

Around Moro, she was like a patient who only felt well in the healer's company; her ailment was deemed benign, curable, but when the healer left, her symptoms returned. It amazed her that her heart had such control over her.

Wurche appreciated that Moro talked to her, because since her marriage, she had almost no access to Etuto and her brothers, except during mealtimes. Just that morning, before she'd left for Salaga, she walked into Etuto's room, where he and his mallam were huddled over a manuscript. She asked him what it was.

"The treaty of friendship we signed with the Germans five years ago," he said, standing up to herd her out. "How are things with Adnan?"

"The one that declared Salaga part of the neutral zone?" Wurche asked, ignoring the question about Adnan.

"Mallam Abu is here. Another time?"

Lately, all her encounters with Etuto fell into that rushed pattern.

*

She went to Salaga and after the class at Jaji's, she met Moro in Maigida's back room.

"Do you spend any time with the Germans?" she asked him. "They signed a treaty to make Salaga and the north a neutral zone and yet they have taken sides. They are protecting the people who fled Salaga after the war."

He leaned forward. A young girl was rasping in the corner. Whenever his slaves were present, Wurche and Moro just talked.

"They signed treaties of friendship with the chiefs in the north, not protection," said Moro. "Kete-Krachi is not in the neutral zone and whoever enters the town is under the protection of the Germans."

"If the Germans say they are friends with us, they shouldn't harbor our fugitives."

"You're confusing friendship and protection. The reason Salaga is not under protection is its location. To the south are the British, to the southeast the Germans, and to the north the French. Nobody wants to go to war against each other. And don't forget the mighty Asante. Everyone wants Salaga and, for now, keeping it neutral pleases everyone."

The slave girl sneezed, an intrusion into their conversation. Before spending time in Maigida's back room, Wurche had never considered what girls like this one, or her childhood friend Fatima, could have gone through to end up as slaves. She hadn't seen this side of the slave raids. In the dank room, they weren't like the slaves who worked on Etuto's farm and went back to their own houses; in the dank room, they were caged.

"Don't you feel for her, for them?" she asked.

Staring at the girl intensely, he said, "I do." Then a beat later, "But destiny placed me on this path. My people believe even a thief has to do his work well."

His parents had sent him, as a child, to work for Shaibu's father. When he'd shown promise in horse riding and archery, the old chief co-opted him for his slave-raiding army. He was sure his destiny would lead him to something. What, he wasn't sure of.

"My grandmother says I'm more interested in the running of Kpembe than I am in the business of Salaga," said Wurche. "And maybe she's right. I don't know much about this. Would Salaga be worse off if we simply stopped the trade?"

"Yes. We would have to replace the slaves with some other trade."

"My father thinks it's the kola nut ... Tell me more. You do the raids, bring these people to Salaga to landlords like Maigida; then what happens?"

"Maigida hosts the people who come in to buy the slaves."

"And the buyers take them where?"

"Some to Asante, but we don't get many Asante buyers anymore. Now, they are taken to the Gold Coast or down the Adirri. Some stay in Salaga and end up working for families like yours."

Of all the options, a slave was probably best off with her family, she thought.

"And after that?"

"I've heard about a big sea. You know the Brazilian Dom Francisco de Sousa?"

Wurche nodded.

"He said the journey to Bahia was worse than the underworld. That the vessel he and a hundred others were stuffed in, something like a large canoe, shook everything in his belly, every single day of the crossing. Nothing stayed down. He said over half of the slaves on the ship died and were thrown into the water, and when he arrived on land again, he was branded with hot brass and sold like a bull."

"How can you continue the raids knowing this?"

He was quiet then said, "This room is nothing compared to when we have to get them from their homes. I try not to leave anyone behind. Most raiders don't take people who are very old, or babies." His voice was a whisper. "They leave them behind and then set everything on fire. Some people think my way is worse, that I make old people suffer on the long journey to Salaga, but I'd rather do that than take their lives. I know I am trying to sound honorable, but I know I am not. I believe I'm working with something bigger than myself."

About five months after her trysts with Moro began, Wurche sat in the dark, dank room, surrounded by the odors of fermenting millet and unwashed bodies. Even Baki had never smelled so bad. She covered her mouth with the collar of her smock to stifle her nausea. The four people were silent, except for one girl whose cough shook the entire room. Voices in the front room: Maigida's, Moro's and a third person's. Moro had brought in a pot of water for his slaves, a small act of kindness she hadn't seen any other raider do. Most of the raiders who came into Maigida's hut shoved their slaves into the back room and didn't look back. And yet, she couldn't reconcile how Moro said he felt for them with how he continued to bring them into such unkindness. Then again, what right did she have to question Moro's morality when her own family insisted on the trade?

The girl coughed, her insides rumbled, and she wheezed incessantly. Wurche pressed her collar harder. Maigida came and dragged off two of the girls without acknowledging Wurche. If he knew who she was, he wasn't letting on.

When the last person had been sold, Wurche felt as if hours had crawled by. Moro apologized and offered to take her to the Hausa suya seller for grilled mutton. Wurche demurred, touched Moro's thigh. He did nothing. Instead, he asked how her teaching was going.

"I prefer racing my horse."

She pressed circles on his thigh, and again he didn't respond. He sat across from her and took her hand in his.

"What's wrong?" she asked.

"I had such a tough time out there. Fewer people are coming up to Salaga. And it's getting too difficult to make money there. The only way I could convince the last buyer to take those two women was by just about giving one of them away. I keep coming here because I know the landlords and the buyers well, but the buyers have stopped coming. Business is better in Kete-Krachi."

Something weary in Moro's voice told her to wait for him to come around, but his next sentence almost brought her to tears.

"I am probably going to stop coming to Salaga and only sell in Kete-Krachi until I can get out of the trade. I wanted to tell you so there'd be no deception or disappointment," he said. "I'll still be coming to Salaga for a few months, while I make the transition, but I don't want you to be disappointed when I'm no longer here."

It was already setting in. Disappointment and a heap of desperation.

"I won't be disappointed," she lied.

"I don't want to be unfair to you."

"Moro," said Wurche, trying to sound brave, digging her fingers into his thigh again. "Everything comes to an end. If you have to go to Kete-Krachi, fine. You're the one who is always mentioning destiny. Let's let it do its work."

He relented and gave in to her caresses.

Their relationship had morphed into glimmers of excitement and bursts of frustration. At least to Wurche. In the back room, their romance grew quiet, shadowy, full of powerful tiny movements that Wurche dreamed about for days after. Dreams she had to keep stretching because most times Maigida's door was locked or Moro wasn't there.

Dramani got his wish to go back to Etuto's farm. He came to Wurche's room to say his goodbyes to her, clutching something wrapped in cotton.

"I didn't use this," he said. "And I hope you won't either."

He handed it to her. She wrapped her hand around the thin cylindrical object. Saliva filled her mouth. It was so copious that she couldn't talk. She dashed out to spit and came back inside. For about a week, she'd been spitting nonstop.

"Why?"

"I don't believe violence is the right way to lead our people. I've seen the damage it does. Also, I'm no good with this thing, made for the sole purpose of taking a life. I hope you use it to shoot something for dinner."

Wurche thanked him, unsure if her brother was really a coward, as some called him, or if he was a wise man ahead of his years. Then she grew sad; she would miss him. Dramani and Moro were the only men who spoke openly and honestly to her, and she was losing them both.

"Wurche," he said before he left. "If you're ever tempted to use it on him, please think about Etuto. You don't want to start a war with Dagbon."

A wise man has to live with fools.
A stone does not walk
But it rolls.

—Gonja Proverb

Wurche

She lifted her smock and studied the calabash extending from her body. The hard knob was almost perfectly round. Another life, growing in her. She fell pregnant around the time Dramani left, four months previously, which was why she had been spitting so much. When she was a child, she asked Mma why men didn't get pregnant. The old lady said it was because Allah created women to be stronger inside, while men were stronger outside. This answer had never satisfied her, especially when *she* was the one lifting heavy objects, not Dramani. Whose child was she carrying? Adnan's with his soft, wide body, or Moro's, cheetah-like and blue?

Moro wasn't in the back room. Once again, she willed herself not to be disappointed. It was an unspoken pact she'd signed with herself when she decided to continue the affair, despite all Moro's warnings (destiny, Kete-Krachi, katcheji): to make no room for disappointment. And yet, as she thanked Maigida and walked out into the bright, blinding afternoon light, she felt a twinge of sadness. Since her belly had swelled up, she hadn't seen Moro at all. She wondered what he'd make of it, of the possibility of the child being his.

As she rode back into Kpembe, Mma, selecting tomatoes from a girl crouched by a basket, looked up in her direction. Wurche dismounted.

"You must stop riding if you want to keep the baby," said Mma. Wurche nodded as the old lady continued her admonishing: Wurche had to stop thinking of just herself. She was delicate now, what if she fell off her horse and lost the baby and couldn't have another one after that? The tomato seller added, in a grating voice, that her elder sister had died in childbirth, but it was because of a family curse that killed all the firstborn daughters on her father's side of the family. Wurche didn't wait to hear the rest of the story.

She lay supine on her bed and exposed her belly. Adnan walked in, his own belly pushing against his smock, and plopped himself on the mat next to her. Beads of sweat dotted his face.

"My pagapulana," he said, palming her belly. My pregnant woman. "Pregnancy looks wonderful on you."

"It's too hot." She brushed away his hand.

"Mma is right. Etuto and I heard her from his room, and we agree. No more horse riding. No more Salaga visits."

Wurche's belly churned. Her body was no longer hers alone and she was going to become its prisoner. "The women need my lessons," she said.

"If you were in Dagbon, my aunts would be pampering you by now. They wouldn't let you even bathe yourself. Someone would wait on you all the time."

Adnan's boasting was annoying her, and she would have bet her horse that he embellished most of the things he said about Dagbon. His pomposity irked her so much that before she could stop herself she said, "If Dagbon is so perfect, go back and let me be."

Adnan flinched and glared at Wurche, as if considering what he should do to her. Since the wedding, she'd carried herself with an indifference that would have come off as shyness to a person as insensitive as Adnan. This was the first time she'd been outwardly nasty to him. As he walked out, she marveled at the grace of his movements, despite his weight.

They would have returned to Dagbon had Etuto not asked that Adnan and some of the soldiers stay to protect him. Then Wurche had fallen pregnant and insisted they stay with her family until the baby could walk. It was one of her small victories. Etuto consented, and so did Adnan.

"It's because she's carrying a boy," Mma said to Adnan, her voice wafting in from outside.

Wurche stared at the door, nose clogging up, tears welling. More often than not, she'd felt trapped by her life, but it had always been external—her father or Mma wouldn't let her do what she liked. Now it was within, too. She didn't want to resent the child making her a prisoner of her own body, but if she was already thinking in those terms, she was losing. She had to fight or she'd go mad.

The next day, she stayed in bed even after the third cock had crowed, even after the whole house could be heard fetching, clanging, chopping. Adnan, a late riser, got up and left the room. He wasn't the kind of man who noticed if a pattern was off. Finally, it was Mma who realized something was wrong and came into the room. She slapped the back of her hand against Wurche's forehead.

"You're not hot, but I was right, wasn't I?" she said. "Going to Salaga has made you sick."

"I'm not leaving this room until the baby is born. Isn't that what you want?"

"Ay, Allah!" exclaimed Mma as she huffed out of the room. She returned with Etuto, Sulemana and Adnan, having briefed them on Wurche's strike. Wurche watched their faces: Sulemana and Etuto looked amused; Mma and Adnan expressed a blend of worry and irritation.

"Wurche," Etuto spoke, "we've agreed that you can continue going to Jaji's, but as soon as you're in your sixth month, you have to stop. You'll go with my messenger from now on. Now, please get out of this room."

It wasn't ideal, but Wurche couldn't help but crack a smile.

"Sheitan," Mma quipped under her breath as she left the room.

Maigida the landlord sat in the front room, across from a hoary white man who had wrapped an indigo scarf around his neck and was crunching into a piece of kola. The white man greeted her in Hausa, studied her as if to unravel from his mind's cobwebs where he'd met her, and went back to talking.

"The new Kpembewura has sent several pleas for Shaibu and the other princes to come back," said the white man. "He's making ardent promises to leave them unscathed, but they say they won't leave." He leaned back, and folded his arms with the smug satisfaction of one who had told a good story.

The landlord turned to Wurche and said, "Sorry, he hasn't come this week. It's been a while. Everything fine?"

"Yes," said Wurche. "I'll wait to see if he shows up."

"The Kpembewura's daughter," the landlord said under his breath, when Wurche was out of sight. "She and this fellow have been coming here for a while. You may have seen him in Kete-Krachi. He's friends with Shaibu. The way royals behave is sickening. Both men and women. A princess can choose a married man if she so desires. It makes them behave badly."

The white man cleared his throat.

Maigida was right about her bad behavior. She had come to Salaga with Etuto's messenger. At Jaji's she'd asked him to wait while she went on foot to the market. Now, she was in Maigida's back room with two lost-looking girls, their wrists chained together, waiting for her lover to show up. It should have bothered her that Maigida knew who she was—he could blackmail her, for instance. But she was more concerned with Moro showing up.

Wurche settled close to the entryway, the better to hear the men's conversation. If this white man had something she could tell Etuto, she might be treated like more than just someone's wife for a change.

"Maigida, the Germans are building in Kete-Krachi," said the white man. "It's already surpassing Salaga in the number of caravans that now go there. The only way your town will be restored is if the Germans are let in."

"You say this because you're German," said the landlord.

"My friend, you've known me now for more than ten years and I've never hidden how I feel about my people. They are hypocrites. But I also know what good they can do. That neutral zone agreement between the Kpembewura, Britain, and Germany is hurting Salaga. Nobody is developing this town because it is neutral. Meanwhile, the British have ulterior motives."

"Ei, Mallam Musa! You always think the British have ulterior motives. And the Germans don't?"

"Mark my words."

So this was *the* Mallam Musa: a white man who had spent so much time in and out of Salaga, he'd been given a local name. She wanted to know why he thought the British had ulterior motives.

Someone walked into Maigida's and Wurche brushed her thoughts aside as one would a pesky mosquito in anticipation of Moro's voice.

She did not hear it.

He didn't show up.

After what had felt like months apart, Moro met her in the back room. His hooked index finger grazed her neck and then his fingers ran down her torso. He grew wide-eyed when his hands bumped over the hard, round protrusion. He flipped up the smock, stared, covered it.

"What is going on?" he said, recoiling and retreating. Wurche couldn't see the light in his eyes. He'd become a solid lump in the darkness. She heard a *thwomp* as he sat on a sack of millet.

"Don't think about it," she said.

He was quiet then asked, "Am I going to be a father?"

The answer was that it was possible. There was no way to be sure. The answer was that it could be his or it could be Adnan's. He seemed to understand that, so didn't push when she didn't answer.

"Now that you're going to be a mother, this is too risky. Even if I am the baby's father, for your honor and your child's sake, let's say it's your husband's child. Now, you have to focus on your husband and child. Wurche, let's end this." She couldn't see his eyes clearly. His tone seemed more regretful than spiteful.

Wurche's throat tightened with swallowed tears. She kneeled before him, and surprised herself by saying, "I can live without him. You, I can't. I need you." She patted the tears on her face. "Please."

He stood up and brusquely tightened the cord of his riding trousers, as if that was his way of cutting himself off, of choking off their relationship. "We both knew this would go nowhere, that it would come to an end. You're married. I'm a nobody. You're in Salaga-Kpembe. I'm in Kete-Krachi."

"You're not a nobody." She reached up to bring him down. She felt as if her heart were being prodded.

"You're a beautiful, powerful woman," he said. "I should never have let things go this far. I'm sorry."

Wurche clutched Moro's shirt and buried her face in his chest. "Please, let's not end this. Moro, I can't breathe without you."

"Once you have that child, you'll forget I even exist," he said, rubbing her back.

Wurche sobbed and hated herself for it. If she'd prepared, she would have appeared steely. She wished she could erase her pleas and coolly agree to the end of the tryst, but her heart throbbed and won out over her desire to appear unperturbed. She felt stripped naked and exposed to all like a slave in the Salaga market. The ache in her heart wanted to push out, extend through her arms, her hands, and inflict pain on Moro, but he clung to her even as she began to squirm out of his grasp. Would the pain go away if she knocked him unconscious? If he ceased to be, would she not feel at all? His very presence seemed to be the reason why she hurt, so why not eliminate it?

Adnan was snoring by her side when she felt the first jabs. At first, they felt like pinches. Then like kicks. They went away. They came back. Stronger. She felt as if she was being twisted from the inside; she thought her hip bones would break through her skin. The yell that poured from her was so loud, so raw, so bloodcurdling, she couldn't believe she was the one screaming. Adnan scrambled awake and ran out after seeing Wurche clutching her belly. The pain subsided and Wurche stood up. She walked to the door, saw that the darkness of night still clung to the trees and huts. She was beside herself with misery and pain. Mma and three older women came to the door, trailed by Adnan.

Wurche was led back to her bed, which someone had covered with white linen. Mma lifted her gown and rubbed shea butter on the hard protrusion that was her belly. One old woman pressed a compress to Wurche's head, and another mashed together dried tree bark, an assortment of roots and a handful of leaves with the long, blade-like look of sorghum. The third boiled a pot of water.

A wave of pain returned, this time surging from her belly to her extremities. Wurche wanted to crawl out of her body. Mma led a calabash of the warm, mashed leaf-bark-root mixture to her lips and said it would strengthen her.

The pain came in pulses and, after what felt like days, Wurche pushed out a giant of a baby. One of the old ladies left the room to share the good news. The women were startled when they heard three gunshots, so close they could have been in the room. They wrapped their arms around each other and waited, hoping their happy day was not going to be marred by the start of another war.

Ululations tore through the fear that had woven its way into the room. In burst all the women of Kpembe, it seemed. Wurche smiled faintly at her admirers, but silently willed them to leave so she could put her head down.

"What were those gunshots?" Mma asked Sulemana, who stood outside the hut. Men were barred for the first eight days.

"Dagbon custom. Three shots for a baby boy."

When the well-wishers left, Wurche held the baby. This strange, beautiful creature had been formed in and come out of her body.

After eight days, Adnan named him Wumpini. God's gift.

Aminah

When the dry, dusty winds blew in from north of Botu, they sapped the earth of moisture, cracked lips, wrung the skin of sweat, and left behind a cold that chilled the bones. The dry winds had arrived in Wofa Sarpong's land, but here they met the wet heaviness of the forest and fought a strange battle in which neither won. It was the girls who suffered. Especially Aminah. This was the second dry season since Wofa Sarpong had brought her to his farm, which meant she had lived there for almost two years. This time, the wind was the kind that Eeyah used to warn about, wind that could cause illness or deform, wind that carried voices with it. Aminah heard Na's voice and Issa's, Eeyah's pipe-ruined voice and the baby's cries.

She sat under the abrofo nkatie tree in front of her room one such windy afternoon, and the voices wouldn't stop. She covered her ears to block them, but they wouldn't go away. She walked and walked till she was in the forest, where the trees broke the wind. Soon, she was in deep and every way she turned was a large tree that looked exactly the same. She had lost the path back to Wofa Sarpong's house. Then she heard voices—real and present ones—and tried to back up, but her foot crunched on a pile of dry leaves. The voices quieted down. Aminah crouched. The patter of feet grew louder. The feet stopped right in front of her, large, each toe crowned with a corn. When she shifted her gaze up, it fell on Kwesi, Wofa Sarpong's eldest son. He carried a basket of red kola and a cutlass. He told his friend to keep walking. He looked at her as one would look at a neighbor's fragrant meal. He grinned and said something as he set down his kola. She hadn't understood him.

Seconds later, Kwesi was on her with all his weight. His stale sweat filled her nostrils. He was spreading apart his cloth and reaching for her. She had come to an uncomfortable arrangement with Wofa Sarpong and he'd never veered off course, but she realized Kwesi was going to finish what his father couldn't or didn't want to. With all the nerve she could muster, she went for his nose, the body part closest to her face, and sank her teeth deep into skin, flesh and cartilage, but she didn't draw blood. Something about spilling someone else's blood stopped her. Still, it hurt him, surprised him; he leapt from her.

She ran in the direction his friend had gone. She ran and ran until she appeared at the edge of Wofa Sarpong's farm. She went into her room and cowered in the corner, the voices in the wind forcing their way in through the cracks in the wall, back to haunt her.

Later that evening, when the wind calmed down, the voices went away, but new, immediate ones mounted. The other girls went to find out why Wofa Sarpong's wives were making more noise than usual, but Aminah stayed on her mat, already aware of what it was about. She curled her body to block out sound, her skin pocked with goose pimples.

They came back in and, unsolicited, Sahada said: "Kwesi said he caught you trying to run away and you bit him. Kwesi's mother says you have to go. Wofa Sarpong will take you away in the morning."

Aminah expected a beating, but that didn't come. Instead, what came that night was deep sleep, with dreams full of warped reminders of the journey that had brought her to this place. Images of Baba in a room with no windows. Images of fire and hangings and dead little boys. They flitted in and out of her mind and she couldn't wake up or change the story, no matter how much she tried.

She woke early. The other girls lay like felled logs carelessly left on the forest floor. Sahada's raspy breathing made her chest rise and fall dramatically. Her arm was flung over another girl's back. Aminah felt strange about leaving them behind, having grown used to them; they had shared a few moments of laughter when they poked fun at Wofa Sarpong and his family, but each of them had held back and, as if knowing their stays would be temporary, none of them had peeled away their outer layers to share their true selves. Aminah walked out of the room, almost colliding with Wofa Sarpong. His hair was overgrown and uncombed, his eyes bloodshot.

"Good," he said. "Let's go."

The look on his face told her she wouldn't be given time to gather her meager belongings. Sacks lay lumped on the ground before his shy donkey—probably the kola Kwesi had been gathering. She helped Wofa Sarpong load them up. He instructed her to cover them with a large red cloth, then they left his home at a brisk pace, as if they were being pursued by an enemy.

After about two hours of traveling, the land grew familiar. The forest was now behind them, the grass grew tall, and baobab and dawadawa trees popped up in bursts. Dawadawa. It was a divisive spice at home. Na's and Eeyah's favorite. Hers, too.

She missed pounding the caked locust beans into dust, as they unleashed their fermented smell into the air, one that Baba and the twins despised. She found that here her memories were less tinged with sadness. She even smiled at the gnarled baobab branches, now bare of leaves and fruit. Wofa Sarpong seemed to have forgotten his troubles, too, because he sang and whistled and slowed down.

"I was going to marry you," he said suddenly, looking back at Aminah. "My wives didn't like it, but give them small time, they understand. Then you try and run away and you bite Kwesi. You work hard, you were respectful. I don't understand, why you do it."

Aminah ignored him. He continued whistling. His good mood seeped through her skin and infected her. Even though what lay ahead was uncertain, she felt calmer than she had in months. When they passed a cowherd who looked like her mischievous neighbor Motaaba, she waved at him.

Wofa Sarpong tried his luck again. "Aminah, you're like my mother. She was the beauty of the village. She come from far away. And then she ran away, to go back. She leave me behind."

Aminah held on to her silence, but that didn't deter him. "Enh, imagine, you leave behind your five-year-old son. Do you do that? Enh?" He went on: "Because you are beautiful and you remind me of my mother, I treat you well. That's not something you can tell people about Wofa Sarpong, that I beat you. I treat you the best."

Up ahead, women in pinks and yellows and greens waded in a wide, muddy river. It reminded Aminah of the water she'd crossed to get to Kintampo, when Hassana had almost been drowned by a panicky girl. Only this was not menacing. They drew nearer. Some women were bent over basins brimming with fish. Others were smoking their catch and the smell went straight through Aminah's nostrils and constricted her belly. She hadn't eaten since the incident with Kwesi. Wofa Sarpong bought two pieces of fish and gave her one. They went along the stream for about ten heartbeats and came to a shallow part of the river guarded by a man on a stool. Wofa Sarpong paid the toll and made Aminah get down. He led the donkey and cart across. As they crossed, Aminah thought of throwing herself into the waters of the river and letting it carry her wherever it wanted to. She gave weight to the thought and swung her body forward, madly rippling the water around her shins. But by the time she'd convinced herself that she could do it they were already on the other shore.

Being back in open space felt good to her spirit. She began to feel as if she'd only just woken up after a long nightmare. She had an existence again. Miyema, they would call it in Botu. Her spirit having a home. And although she didn't know how far away home was, or if home still existed, something about this place was pleasing to her being. Meanwhile, dust whirled around them and Wofa Sarpong had covered his mouth with a rag. Aminah was pleased that it didn't carry voices this time. It was dry and light, the way the harmattan winds were supposed to be. She was sure they were closer to Botu than ever before.

They traveled for hours. The sun began its descent, painting the sky with wide strokes in pinks, oranges and purples. Wofa Sarpong unwrapped his cloth and threw it back over his shoulder. He couldn't stop fidgeting.

"This take too long," he said, as the sky grew dark.

They made quick stops to water the donkey and rest. She imagined that if their stops lasted any longer, Wofa Sarpong would want to continue their dance, only this time his wives weren't around so nothing would stop him from finishing the act. She slept on top of the kola and, at dawn, Wofa Sarpong yelled, waking her. "Things change. No look right."

They had been traveling for two days and still they plodded on. The donkey cart dipped down an incline, and the silhouettes of houses came into view.

"Ah, at last," said Wofa Sarpong. "But things change too much. This is a ghost town."

As they closed in on the village, the sun crept higher. It was the biggest village Aminah had ever seen, despite what Wofa Sarpong was mumbling. There were hundreds, maybe thousands of buildings, many broken down and covered with soot, huge trees surrounding them. The minarets of a mosque rose as high as the trees. A flock of guinea fowl flew by, making her ache badly for Botu.

"Ah, but these people destroy Salaga," said Wofa Sarpong as they went down into the valley, flinging his hand in the air, as if the town were his creation.

This was Salaga? From Baba's stories, Aminah had dreamt of towers and colorful buildings and thousands of people coming and going.

They squeezed through a narrow road the color of a red kola nut, while a dog with swollen teats grazing the ground strolled by. The muezzin's call rang out, and soon chatter, clanging metal and crowing cocks took over. They wove through even narrower streets, which Aminah wasn't convinced could fit a donkey cart, but they plowed through. They passed a dry, red flat where men and women were spreading brown squares of cloth on the crusty earth, and they stopped in front of a rectangular building. It had two entrances and two windows in front, with steps leading up to the bigger entrance. Wofa Sarpong got down and helped Aminah off the cart. He looked at her with longing and sadness.

"Why you bite Kwesi?"

Aminah was sure her answer didn't matter.

A tall man with the darkest skin she'd ever seen walked by, trailed by a group of men and women tied together. Aminah shuddered as she remembered the horsemen who'd abducted her. The man stopped next to the building they were standing by. He smiled at Wofa Sarpong and Aminah, and went in with his brood through the larger door.

"Ah, this man paaa," said Wofa Sarpong querulously. "He not see I get here first?"

But Wofa Sarpong didn't shift a foot. He stayed by the donkey cart until the tall man exited without his people. As they were heading in, the tall man paused to whisper to Wofa Sarpong and his eyes met Aminah's. She broke the gaze. She could tell he pitied her. Wofa Sarpong nodded slowly at first, then rapidly. A smile spread across his face and he stepped aside for the tall man to re-enter the building. The man came back out, shook hands with Wofa Sarpong, looked at Aminah warmly, and then went on.

Inside the building, the room was dark and cool. Cowskins were spread on the floor and a man sat on a brown hide, placing cowry shells on the balancing plate of a pair of scales.

"Ah, Wofa Sarpong," said the man. At the other end of the room, a cloth covered a doorway. Four windows framed the front and sides of the room, and not much else filled the space. The man spoke in Hausa. "I'm happy you've come. Why has it been so long?"

"Ah, these plenty wars your people do. It's not safe. And if they know I'm Asante man, I can lose my head."

"But we pay more for your kola up here," said the man, pulling up the sleeves of his white robe. "This is the beauty our friend is getting."

"*Your* friend," said Wofa Sarpong. "I just meet him. Outside. Now now now."

"Why are you selling such a precious gem?"

"Long story. I need the money."

"You don't waste time at all. Well, he said he would pay me, so I'll buy her from you and he'll pay me later."

"He mention a good price," said Wofa Sarpong. "You trust him? He seem like good man. Somebody else would make deal with me, cut you landlord out."

"Yes, I've known him a long time. Always pays me my dues. Let me take her to the back," said the man, standing up. He was just as short as Wofa Sarpong. Aminah wondered how much she was worth, but the man, perhaps sensing her desire to know this, shoved her through the cloth into a room that smelled of fermenting millet dough. On sacks and on the floor were the people the tall man had herded in. Before them was a small clay pot of water. They looked like she had when she first arrived in Kintampo: dehydrated and dusty. She nodded at them and found a small space of the floor to settle on. She strained to hear the rest of the conversation, but Wofa Sarpong and his friend's voices were muted.

So the tall man was buying her. And the rest of these people? Aminah counted eight. One old lady, four girls, two men, one boy. Where were they going to end up? Wofa Sarpong stuck his head through the doorway and waved at her.

"Why you want to run away?" he asked again.

"I wasn't running away. Your son wanted to finish what you started."

He cocked his head to the side, then retreated. She felt slight panic when he disappeared. As unhappy as she had been, his place had been stable, better than when she had traveled with the horsemen. Her fingernails found her teeth. The skin at the tip of her fingers grew raw.

Throughout the day, the man in the white robe, Maigida— as Aminah had heard people address him—came in and took people out. Some returned, others didn't. Late in the afternoon, he took those remaining to relieve themselves behind his house, where a few trees were clustered and a wild bush was blossoming despite the dryness.

Soon they were down to three: Aminah, the old woman and another girl.

The old woman, curled up in a corner, didn't say a word. Aminah was surprised the horsemen had not left her behind. The girl bounded over to Aminah as soon as she realized the front room was quiet.

"You're beautiful," said the girl. Her language sounded like Aminah's, but where Aminah used an "l" the girl used an "r." When Aminah thanked her, the girl was shocked, then said she was happy they could understand each other. At first Aminah strained to make meaning of her sentences, but soon adjusted. The girl was called Khadija.

"The way you're beautiful," she said, "I'm sure you're expensive, not like me. I'll stay here for a week before they sell me. My father used to say I was so ugly that if I went to hell, even Sheitan would turn me away." She smiled and her eyes crinkled. Aminah found her pleasant. Her eyes were large and set a wide distance from each other. Three parallel diagonal marks scarred either cheek. Her nose and mouth were small. Maybe that was the problem, that her features were too small on her face; they should have been more pronounced. But Aminah didn't think she was ugly. "You'll be out of here in less than a day. I'm sure he's saving you for someone with a lot of money."

"I've already been sold," said Aminah.

"I told you!" beamed Khadija.

Aminah thought about the man who'd bought her. She had no idea what she was going to do for him, but his look had reassured her. She asked Khadija how long she'd been a captive. She couldn't bring herself to use the word "slave" because it would apply to her, too. She didn't think of herself as a slave.

"Three years ago my father gave me up to pay a debt. It was fine, because it was to a friend of his, and I knew his children. I was like one of the family. I was even going to marry one of his sons." Khadija yawned, and Aminah followed. Khadija roared in amusement. "Imagine, ugly me, married! I was very happy. And then that raider came and set fire to the farm. Ah, I'm tired!"

"The tall one?" asked Aminah. He'd seemed so kind.

She nodded and stretched. "It's nice to be sleeping in a room again. But you are so beautiful. It's not fair."

Aminah admired whatever it was that made Khadija upbeat. She'd lost as much as Aminah had, could have suffered more, but she did not wear her pain. She didn't dwell. Aminah couldn't be as cheerful and she didn't feel beautiful, hadn't in a long time. Moreover, she had never known how to respond when people said she was beautiful. Otienu had carved her body. He could have chosen a tree for her spirit. She didn't pick her body or create her beauty, so it felt almost dishonest to thank people for something she didn't do. She said as much to Khadija.

"Let's exchange our bodies, then," said Khadija, slapping her thighs and laughing.

The curtain parted and Maigida set a large calabash before them. Khadija and Aminah called out to the old woman, and when she ignored them, the two girls made for the bowl like hyenas and grabbed mounds of tuo coated in the slime of ayoyo-leaf soup. Aminah had missed eating real tuo, made of millet, not Wofa Sarpong's green plantain tuo. Wofa Sarpong's family also ate cocoyam leaves, which she'd found bland, with none of ayoyo's stretch and earthiness. Khadija sucked on her knuckles when she was done. They left a third of the tuo for the old woman and pushed it towards her. In the outer room, they heard Maigida talking to people. One of the voices was high-pitched.

"Ah, I'm so pleased you have kola now," said the voice.

"We got in a fresh supply from Kintampo," said Maigida.

"Thanks be to Allah. I was going to have to continue on to Kete-Krachi if I didn't get some here."

Khadija looked content.

When Aminah asked Khadija about her fiancé, she smiled so brightly Aminah felt like the world was all right. Her intended, as Khadija called him, was born to two very tall parents, but he came out squat. And she was convinced that that was why they liked each other: because their families made them feel like outsiders. Khadija was tasked with making sure the babies in the house slept, but when they saw her, all they wanted to do was play. One day, it was too hot in the house, so she took them to the big tree outside. They were irritable and didn't want to sleep, and she was frustrated to the point that she considered leaving them and running back to her parents' village. Then, she heard a voice singing. The children did too. They sat up, quieted down, and one by one, they fell asleep. When the last one was sleeping, the singer showed his face. Khadija hugged him and from that day, they became best friends. Just before the raiders came, he asked her to be his wife.

Aminah wanted to ask Khadija if he had survived the raid, but wondered if it was an insensitive question, so she said, "Did he come with you?"

"I am so thankful to Allah that he had gone to my parents' village to present the dowry," she said. "No matter where I go, he'll find me or I'll find him."

The old lady snorted. Aminah wondered if the timing was coincidental or if she'd been listening to them. She had seemed ignorant of their language. And she hadn't shifted from her fetal position.

"Something Allah has meant to be, no one can destroy," said Khadija. Aminah was surprised Khadija kept saying Allah and not Otienu. It meant her people had become people of the book. Not in Botu. Her people had refused to convert. That was one of the reasons Eeyah's parents had had to move. "What about you? I'm sure people were lining up outside your door to ask for your hand."

Aminah shook her head. "Only one. A wrinkled old man came to greet my family just before I got kidnapped."

"I don't believe you!" Her eyes opened wide. "Beautiful girl like you." She clucked and turned her lips down. "Then people are truly blind."

Khadija talked and talked and talked. Aminah went through moments when she wanted her to shut up so she could make sense of where she was, but mostly she was glad for her company. Loneliness would have plunged her into self-pity.

By the time Aminah woke up the next day, Khadija was gone. Was she to be resigned to a life in which people simply disappeared? Now, it was just her and the old lady. Her bladder was bursting, so she sucked in her fear and made for the outer room. Maigida led her outside, to the bush behind his building, and he didn't shackle her as he'd done with the big group. He stood off to the side, paying little attention to her. Beyond the bush was open space that sloped up. Its disadvantages were many: running up the slope would be tough and Aminah could easily be shot.

"You're taking too long," said Maigida.

When she went back inside, the old lady hadn't moved. She didn't flinch when Aminah touched her, planning to shake her awake, but her skin was cool and dry.

"Maigida!"

"Ah ah! What now?"

"The old lady is dead."

He took his time and shuffled in. He bent over and pressed her wrist. Then he sucked his teeth deeply. He left and returned with two boys. One placed his palms under the woman's shoulders and the other grabbed her legs. They hoisted her up and out of the room without a word. Maigida came back in to inspect the area where she'd died and when he was satisfied he headed for the outer room.

"When will I leave?" asked Aminah.

"When your buyer returns."

Maybe it was his height, or his baby face, round with small eyes, that encouraged her to keep asking him questions.

"Will I sleep here alone?"

"More will come."

She was more worried about the old lady's spirit. She hadn't died happily. What if she became an evil spirit walker and returned to haunt the room?

A few people were brought in, but they were all sold by the end of the day.

Aminah lay awake on a bag of millet that night, listening to hyenas and jackals outside, and scratchy sounds inside. She fell asleep around dawn.

Days ran into days and Aminah remained cloistered in the back room. By the fourth or fifth day Maigida said, "I don't know where your master is but he's costing me money."

The next day, Maigida grabbed her wrists and dragged her out of his building. The first cock hadn't even crowed. They marched behind rows of huts, past the large mosque with its tall tower, and as he led her along narrow streets, Aminah stumbled, her stomach curdling from the stink of rubbish and decay. And fear. They were leaving the village, it seemed. They left the huts behind for tall grass and shea butter trees. Maigida walked so fast, skipping over objects, that she almost fell into a well, twice. A jackal scurried off as they approached a bushy area. Then other people came into view, gathered around a number of small ponds. Girls were washing themselves while men with long-barreled guns stood guard. Maigida ordered her into a pond that held only one girl. Aminah peeled off her wrapper and lowered herself into the water. Shivering, she washed herself. The water had barely touched her skin when it began to evaporate with the harmattan dryness. As the girls finished they climbed out of their ponds and were met by women clutching huge calabashes of shea butter. Aminah got out and an unsmiling woman gave her a dollop of shea butter, which she spread on her arms and belly and down her legs. The woman gave her another dollop. It was too much, but she jutted her chin forward, instructing that Aminah add another layer of oil. When satisfied, the woman signaled to Maigida. Before Aminah could pick up her wrapper, Maigida grabbed her wrist and they went back in the direction from which they'd come. Aminah pictured her discarded cloth, bunched carelessly on the grass, and wished she could go back and get it. But Maigida's grasp was unrelenting. Instead of heading to his building, they stopped at the open market just before it. He took Aminah to a tree, shackled her ankles, and pointed to a large stone. She tried to make eye contact with him, but he wouldn't look at her.

"Please," Aminah begged. *Please, clothe me. Please, not this.* He said nothing else. Other raiders brought their captured people and sat them by her. She bent her head and saw her breasts, her black bushy triangle. This was the most exposed she'd felt since her exile from Botu. Even when she'd had on a wrapper, she'd attracted people like Wofa Sarpong and the turbaned man of the caravans. What would her nakedness bring? What had happened to the tall man who was to buy her? Why was nothing good coming to her?

She slunk to the ground, wrapped her hands around her legs and buried her head in the pocket between her knees. *When will this end*, she wanted to scream. Instead, she rocked back and forth, trying to ignore the sun's rays roasting her back.

Wurche

The baby grew and grew and as soon as it could roll over, Wurche was ready for life to go back to normal. She carried Wumpini into Etuto's quarters where, for the first time in a long time, he was on his own. Rifles, muskets, bows and arrows were dotted like stars on his wall. In every corner sat a canister of gunpowder. She was worried that, with one false move, her father would be blown to pieces, as had happened to El Hadj Umar Tall, commander of the Toucouleur Empire whose stock of gunpowder exploded and killed him. Etuto had liked the comparison to the man of valor, but said his enemies were far too many for him to let his guard down. The baby stared wide-eyed at his grandfather. Etuto took him, flung him in the air and caught him. Wumpini shrieked in delight.

Wurche laid down her agenda. "I want to join you the next time you meet the Germans and the British," she said. "I'll listen and tell you what I think when they're gone. Already, I know the Germans are looking to poach the Salaga traders and have them go to Kete-Krachi."

Etuto returned Wumpini to her and pointed to him.

"He spends more time with Mma than he does with me," said Wurche.

"I hoped motherhood would cure you," said Etuto. "Aren't you better off teaching with Jaji?"

"Etuto, you admitted I did you a favor by marrying Adnan. You can't keep dismissing me."

"Fine. But this information is not new. They are calling Kete-Krachi 'New Salaga.' The Germans are working with the escaped princes and installing a new king of Salaga there. They just want to confuse the traders."

"I know your strategy is going after the escaped princes," said Wurche. "But, I don't think that's where you should focus. It should be on the treaties you're signing with the white men. I heard a white German trader in Salaga ..."

"Mallam Musa?"

"Yes, he said the British have ulterior motives. He might have said this because he's German, but there was something earnest in his voice."

"The princes have to be stopped because *they* are the ones trying to lure Salaga's traders to Kete-Krachi. And people like novelty. Even if I am trying to teach them a lesson, so what? We have a saying that if someone offends you, you retaliate." Etuto gestured to a pouf. "Sit. You must be tired from carrying this one around."

Wurche sat, and bounced Wumpini on her lap.

"You *are* right about one thing," said Etuto. "The Europeans are playing a game I don't understand. We declared a neutral zone with both Germans and the British, but for some time now, it has begun to feel as if they are competing with each other and not working with us. The British keep bringing me wonderful gifts. The Germans strike me as a bit cold when they come. They never stay with us or drink our beer. I don't know what their plan is. But, Wurche, I don't want you heartbroken. Before you get involved, ask your husband for permission."

Adnan would say no, but she wouldn't let that stop her. She asked why the agreements with the Europeans were important.

"They protect us from the Asante first and foremost, then the French, who would also like to take Salaga. It's all about control, Wurche. Whoever has control of Salaga is most powerful. My goal is to have the Europeans come here to trade directly. No Asante middlemen. The Europeans want the same thing. If they come directly, people will come back to Salaga from Mossi, from Kano, from Yorubaland. Salaga will get back in shape. But *we* have to stay in charge. Kete-Krachi is for the Germans, and the British have the Gold Coast."

"Honestly, these treaties do not sound beneficial to us."

"They are. In fact, since the Europeans defeated the Asante, most of us have been able to sleep. Those days when we had to send over thousands of slaves in tribute were terrible. Your neighbor could sell you out just like that."

Wurche wanted to tell her father that he was still enabling the trade, that he was never in danger of ending up a slave. She wanted to describe the people in Maigida's room. But what solution could she offer to replace the lucrative trade? She hadn't thought that far. Her father watched her. The whites of his eyes were now gray. He hadn't had any episodes of staying in his room since he'd become Kpembewura. Wurche prayed he'd stay strong, because as soon as people found out that he had a weakness, they would exploit it. Etuto must also have been appraising her, because he said suddenly, "With all the changes happening, our alliance with Dagbon needs to remain as solid as possible."

"Then let me help you," Wurche said.

"Ask your husband first. All he needs is a drink now and then and he'll lighten up." He reached for his favorite gourd. "The fellow is too stiff."

Wumpini, round and squishy, lay on his back, legs kicking, toes curled. A line of drool slipped down his cheek. Wurche wiped it. She stuck a finger in his fist and he greedily grabbed it. His mouth rolled into an oval, as if he were trying to say something. She marveled at his helplessness, that she, too, had once been like him. She saw none of herself in him, but Mma insisted his gestures came from her. She picked him up, lifted her smock, and led his mouth to her nipple. His mouth swallowed her entire breast.

Adnan burst in with such force that the door's curtain fluttered behind him. Wurche briefly regarded him, saw he was in no need of her, and continued to feed Wumpini.

"It's dawned on me why men marry more than one wife." He paused, and when she wasn't forthcoming, said, "It's because after children are born wives have no more time for their husbands. It's Islam that has spoiled things. My great-grandfather had as many wives for every child that was born." He laughed, clearly in a good mood. This was the time to strike.

"Did you enjoy shooting with Sulemana?" Topics had to be broached delicately, as if they were a bowl of eggs.

"Your brother is gifted with the bow and arrow. He caught a few guinea fowl. I missed every shot."

"He taught me to shoot, but I can say with pride that I'm better than he is."

"I find that hard to believe. Sule is extraordinary."

Wurche cringed at the name "Sule." No one called him that. Why did even his innocent words irk her? She shifted Wumpini to the other breast, so the baby's wide eyes would be in view. Then she patted the space beside her. Adnan sat.

"Can I have your permission to work with Etuto?"

Adnan sighed. "And who'll take care of Wumpini?" He flicked Wumpini's cheek with a curled index finger, then stood up and stretched like a fat cat. He took off his shirt. His belly hung over his trousers. "I'm heading to Dagbon in two nights and I'll be back in two weeks, inshallah. When we move back there, I'm sure your restlessness will be cured. My aunts will have plenty for you to do. In the meantime, take care of Wumpini."

A familiar sentiment of panic rose in Wurche's throat. She'd grown so comfortable with having him around that she'd forgotten their being there was temporary. Women moved into their husband's homes, not the other way around. Only the war in Salaga had made Adnan move in with them.

One thick thigh emerged from a trouser leg, then the other. His movements, fluid and surprisingly nimble, made him seem at home in his body. As she watched him with melding repulsion and fascination, she consoled herself with having negotiated for Wumpini to walk before moving to Dagbon. She prayed that he would be like Sundiata, the Lion of Mali, and spend the first seven years of his life crawling.

*

Wurche was shaken awake roughly. When she opened her eyes, Adnan was crouching before her. She couldn't believe two weeks had gone by so fast. Disoriented, she looked about. Wumpini was sleeping with his buttocks in the air. It had to be about two hours after midnight. Adnan unraveled her wrapper and rubbed his stubbly chin on her belly. Since Wumpini had been born, Wurche had managed to keep him at bay. Now, she tried to protest, pushed his hands off her thighs, but he barely heard her as he hoisted up her legs and pushed himself into her. At first she swallowed each thrust as it came, but as he grew more agitated, a bubble of heat formed in her belly and spread through her womb, through her legs. She kicked, and her heel made contact with something hard but organic. He staggered back, holding his forehead, and regarded her for a second. Then before she could stop him, he smacked her across the face. For the first seconds, the slap silenced the world. Then the pain rang in her ear. He slapped her again.

"It's normal for a man to want his wife after being away from her," said Adnan. "It's normal for a husband and wife to have relations. What is not normal is for a wife to hit her husband. You pushed me, Wurche. You've never considered what I sacrificed to be here. That I also didn't want this. That I might have also been forced to marry you. You haven't even tried to get to know me."

He left the room. Wurche curled into a ball and watched the baby, still asleep, despite the commotion.

*

In front of Jaji's hut a staggering man trolled drunken tunes. The town was in ruins, but its spirit remained strong.

"Salaam alaikum," said Wurche.

"Salaam alaikum," sang the man. "Alaikum salaam!"

"Alaikum salaam," responded Jaji, parting the curtain before her door, and shooing away the madman, who bowed and took the road to Kpembe, on which Wurche had just come.

Jaji welcomed Wurche. Just as Etuto's quarters were distinctly his—one could almost taste the metal in his room—so were Jaji's. Her room smelled of incense and old paper. Books and rolled manuscripts were strewn across a cowskin. She put away a manuscript she'd spread open on the cowskin and told Wurche the women had not stopped asking of her. Wurche smiled sadly. After the fight with Adnan, he'd reported her behavior to Etuto, who had said she should defer to her husband and bide her time. The only reason she was allowed to come to Salaga was that the men of the house had gone to a meeting and Mma needed salt.

Jaji, head inches from the raffia ceiling, studied Wurche as if to unlock the things that went unsaid. It was a trick Jaji used to get her interlocutor to say more. Wurche knew better. Jaji went into the corner of the room and riffled through her collection of bowls and calabashes, dropping a metal plate in the process. She scooped water from a large clay pot and handed it to Wurche with a bowl of kola.

"I'm happy to see you," said Jaji. "Because, sadly, my stay in Salaga is coming to an end. I am moving to Kete-Krachi. The imam has already moved. He has called for me to join him there."

Wurche told her that Adnan, convinced that Wumpini would walk soon, was planning for them to move to Dagbon. "I don't like Dagbon." It was the first time she'd admitted this even to herself. She swallowed a large drink of water as her teacher observed her. "I am suffocating, Jaji. If I stay in this marriage, I'll lose my mind."

"Why? What has happened?"

"It's simple: there is no love between us. Or maybe it's me. I don't like him and I don't think I can grow to love him."

Jaji said nothing. The silence in the room grew heavy. Jaji asked Wurche if Adnan had insulted her. Wurche said no. If he had insulted her father. Wurche said no. If he was a drunkard. Wurche said no. If he beat her. Wurche told her about the night when she'd kicked him.

"I'm sorry to hear that," said Jaji. "Let's read what the Koran says."

Jaji went to her well-worn Koran and lifted the pages delicately.

"Here's one." She read, "'Those who intend to divorce their wives shall wait three months; if they change their minds and reconcile, then Allah is Forgiver, Merciful. If they go through with the divorce, then Allah is Hearer, Knower.' This is for men." She flipped the pages. "Listen. The good, educated Muslim woman should also be a good wife," said Jaji. "I can't find the passage, but it sounds like you are unable to be a good wife to Adnan. If I remember correctly, the verse says that a woman can divorce her husband because he beats her or forces her to do forbidden acts."

"I prefer that *he* divorce me."

"Why?"

"I married him to strengthen our alliance with Dagbon. My father wants to do everything to keep that link as tight as possible. If I divorce him, I'll have to leave Kpembe and Salaga and hide in a well."

Jaji had been married once, but her husband had died from smallpox. Something told Wurche that her teacher was happier widowed. Wurche excused herself. She had to get to the market and return to Kpembe before Adnan and Etuto got back.

"Pray over it," said Jaji, as Wurche untied Baki.

They waved goodbye, and Wurche made for the big afternoon market, wondering, as she had all the way from Kpembe to

Salaga and even as she spoke to Jaji, whether Moro was in the back room. She'd told herself she'd visit her teacher, buy salt, and return to Kpembe, but a knot had grown in her belly and she was convinced that the only way to uncoil it was to go the back room. Just to make sure he wasn't there.

When she and Fatima had played their game, she hadn't thought it inherently wrong, but she knew if they were seen, they would get in trouble, which is exactly what had happened when Mma caught them. Not long after that, she and Jaji studied a poem about the path of truth. When asked how *she* stayed on the elusive path of righteousness, Jaji said, "The text says, 'Stop straying from the path.' The word 'straying' is key here. It recognizes that we're human and that, sometimes, we do things continually, over and over, until we get them right. We all get more than one chance. I usually just pray and stop repeating my mistakes."

Wurche inched Baki forward, willing herself to change her mind. Saying a prayer of sorts. *Stop repeating your mistakes.* What would she say to Moro when she saw him? Would she bring up the baby? *Stop repeating your mistakes.* She cut across the road that would take her back to Kpembe and considered going home, making up some excuse to Mma about the salt. But that became a passing thought, because she kept on, crossed the ruined mosque, entered the market, and stopped before the hut she and Moro had made their lover's den. *Stop repeating your mistakes.* She tied Baki to the tree next to the building and made for the door.

"Salaam alaikum!" she shouted, but no one responded.

The door was locked. Disappointment met relief. She went back to her horse, her trusty Baki, and began untying the knot she'd made.

"Ah ha!" shouted a voice, accompanied by three loud claps. It was Maigida, Moro's landlord friend. She'd never seen him outside or standing up. He was about half her size, with ashy skin. He needed sun. "Your man-friend left his slave here and hasn't come back for her. It's costing me money. Feeding her alone ..."

"Lower your voice," Wurche said through gritted teeth. She tightened the knot. "And don't call him my man-friend."

"I'm sorry. You see ... you can't trust anyone in this town anymore. He was one of the last trustworthy ones."

"When was the last time you saw him?"

"A week ago." So Moro was still coming to Salaga. "Come inside." They went into the cold room and he offered Wurche a cowskin. "He bought this girl from another of my buyers. He was thrilled, but now he's left her here and I've received no message from him."

"Where did he go?"

"He said Kete-Krachi, and that he would return, latest, in three days. It's day seven. I could make a lot of money selling her to someone else. I'm a good man, but my patience is wearing thin."

Moro sold people. He didn't buy them, thought Wurche. Why was he buying this girl? "Show her to me."

"Follow me, please."

They walked to the market. Laughter, loud conversations, drumbeats, dogs barking, singing, butchers hacking at meat, bells ringing. Everywhere Wurche turned, there was a flurry of activity. It amazed her how resilient human beings were. Things were broken, but life went on. Maigida greeted continually and stopped before a group of people chained to each other.

"This one." He pointed to a girl a few years younger than Wurche. She looked up at Maigida, her expression accusing him of something. Her skin was reddish like the laterite in the market, her hair was plaited in cornrows, her haughty nose came to a point, her lips were full and her breasts were small and perky. Wurche's heart contracted and the feeling slid into her belly. For seconds, words abandoned her. The girl was beautiful. What had Moro planned to do with her?

"I'll take her," Wurche said, nauseous. From spending time with Moro, the whole idea of slavery had grown questionable to her and, yet, in a heartbeat, without pausing, she'd offered to buy someone.

Maigida's face changed. He didn't seem pleased, but said nothing. Then it hit Wurche. The Kpembewura was usually given unsold slaves as gifts. Maigida probably thought she was asking to be given the girl for free. When the old Kpembewura was alive, Shaibu and the other princes picked slaves with impunity, leaving many landlords fuming. Wurche did not want to be anything like Shaibu. She rummaged in the pocket of her smock. She had cowries for Mma's salt and a few more she carried whenever she came to Salaga, which she seldom spent.

"How much?" she asked.

Disposition changed, Maigida clapped his hands and led Wurche by the arm.

"Let's go back inside to discuss price," he said. "We don't sell out in the open."

"How much were you selling her to Moro for?"

"Well, you know he's a friend ..."

"Fine. Tell him I outbid him. No need to make the process long."

Moro was buying her at 250 cowries. Girls were usually 400. The landlord settled for 300. He started talking about how some of his clients enjoyed bargaining for bargaining's sake. Some of them spent entire afternoons there just to get the upper hand. He shut up when he saw that Wurche was looking at the door.

There was the problem of how to transport the girl to Kpembe. She would have to ride with Wurche. Mma was going to have several fits. No salt. *A slave on a horse.* Mma said once that if a commoner sat on a horse, its lifetime was shortened.

The landlord went back and unshackled the girl. She stood as tall as Wurche. The pain returned to Wurche's chest. It was pure, uncontaminated jealousy. And more. Something like attraction.

"What does she speak?"

"Tell her," said the landlord, but the girl continued to stare at him with eyes that condemned him for some wrongdoing. "Hausa," he said. "Some Twi, I believe."

"Very well," said Wurche. "What's your name?"

The girl looked at Wurche, didn't say anything at first. Her eyes darted up and down as she studied her, deciding whether or not to speak.

"Aminah," she said, finally.

Aminah

The woman with the short hair and man's smock walked Aminah across the market and bought her a cotton smock, which Aminah gratefully put on. They moved wordlessly. The boyish woman strode ahead and Aminah followed, befuddled. The only clear thing was that the man who was supposed to have bought her hadn't shown up, and Maigida had sold her to the boyish woman. They stopped before a horse with a coat so black and shiny she was sure she would catch her reflection in it.

"Up," barked the boyish woman in Hausa, but Aminah stood still.

Before Aminah could think of how to get up, the boyish woman shoved her against the horse, grabbed her waist as if she were a child, and hoisted Aminah up with her shoulders. The woman's fingers pressed into Aminah's rib cage so she scrambled up to end the discomfort. The boyish woman then climbed up in front like a monkey, took Aminah's hands and clasped them around her waist. They set off so fast that Aminah was sure she would fall, but the woman had control of the creature. The roughness of the smock scratched Aminah's skin and the woman's leather bag poked her stomach, but fear had seized her throat. They climbed up out of the valley and the sand jagged into rocky land, with spurts of tall grass.

Aminah imagined that once they breasted the top of the incline, she would look down and see Botu. She would jump off the horse, run, taste the soil, and then return to embrace this woman who'd saved her. But when they plateaued, they met large trees lining a golden-brown path. A gust of wind blew through, scattering fallen leaves. It was not Botu.

"Get down," ordered the woman.

It was quite a height. The boyish woman leapt down and reached for Aminah, beckoning her down. With much trepidation, Aminah held on to the woman's outstretched hand, but still couldn't jump, her body glued to the horse. After a loud, annoyed sigh, the woman tugged her with such force that she fell off. The woman got back on her horse with ease and trotted ahead. Aminah dusted off the red dirt and followed, surprised that she'd been allowed to ride the horse and now suddenly wasn't wanted. Was it because of the odor of her body?

Fifteen minutes later, they arrived in another town, smaller and more solemn than Salaga. Missing were the sounds that gave Salaga its heartbeat, its special flavor: the muezzin's call, dogs barking, a drunk—always a drunk—singing his way home, bells, drums, lazy cocks crowing after the morning had already begun, more muezzin calls, the voices of people buying and selling, loud laughter, continuing until evening.

Girls were playing outside a hut and Husseina and Hassana flitted back into Aminah's mind. Had they found each other? She hoped she would see them again. She thought she had numbed herself of feeling—happiness, sadness, nostalgia—but seeing these girls made her realize she wasn't at all numb. She missed her family. She willed herself to look away from the children, who were now watching her, the same way they'd stared in Botu every time a new person came by. As they continued on, the gazes of the girls burned into her back.

They stopped before a bright white house with two big rocks flanking an entrance, through which the woman went. She dismounted, landing on a smooth floor made of a thousand tiny mirror shards, reflecting light on everything. She led the horse into a room to the left of the entrance. Aminah craned her neck and saw three more horses. The boyish woman had to be wealthy, thought Aminah. Several huts lined the courtyard, and Aminah was led into a small one with a blue-and-white striped curtain draped in front of its door. The woman called out in a language Aminah had heard for the first time in Salaga. She preferred it to the language of Wofa Sarpong—this one almost sounded as if a gong were being beaten when people spoke. Out shuffled an old woman. She was round in a way Eeyah was not. Her eyes, nose, even her mouth were round. And yet, she made Aminah think of her grandmother. She decided that all old people look alike. Their cheekbones, their jaws, their pleated necks. The two women exchanged heated words, then the boyish woman turned to Aminah and spoke in Hausa.

"Mma, my grandmother," she said. The old lady welcomed Aminah into her room, where she sank into a bed raised with blocks of sand. Between the old woman and the wall lay a sleeping baby. The baby was curled like a leaf and looked so peaceful, Aminah found herself strangely envious of him. The two women's voices went up again and, as if they remembered the baby at the same time, they stopped speaking in unison and watched Aminah, whose feet fused with the ground. Then the old lady spoke.

"You're here to help Wurche, my granddaughter, take care of her baby," she said. The baby was four months old, and

Aminah's tasks were to bathe him, feed him, put him to bed. When he slept, she was to help around the house, cooking and cleaning. "Rest today. There's plenty to do in the coming days."

Aminah couldn't believe the boyish woman had had a baby. She was a pole. She also wondered, as they left Mma's hut for the one next to it, when someone like Wofa Sarpong would appear. Wurche unlocked the door and inside were a mat, an army of pots and pans coated with dust, and piles of sand gathered along the base of the walls. She pushed the window open. The tinny smell of metal grew stronger the longer they stayed in the room. Wurche showed Aminah to the cooking area, an open shed with metal pans, clay pots and utensils piled on a low, wide table. Under the table were brooms, mats, hoes and digging tools, more pots and pans. Wurche left Aminah with a broom and returned with arms overflowing with clothes, which Aminah presumed were to be washed.

"They are yours," said Wurche. "I've never worn them and never will."

Who were Wurche and her people? They were treating Aminah too well. How long would the hospitality last? She took out the mat in the room and shook it out; crusty bits of dried grass broke into her hand. As she returned the broom to the kitchen, a man limped out of the hut across the way. He came towards her, saying something in the language Mma and Wurche had spoken. Aminah shook her head. He tried Hausa.

"I haven't seen you here before," he said.

Aminah said she was looking after Wurche's baby. He said he was Wurche's older brother, Sulemana. And if Aminah needed anything, to go to him for help. She was sure she would do no such thing. The kind treatment was agreeable, but it was as if she were wearing borrowed clothes that were too small. Or like she was holding her breath, and exhaling would make everything fall apart. She stared at her fingers, raw after repeated biting. Back in the room she'd been given, she closed her eyes, her thoughts all over the place. What had happened to the man who intended to buy her? How long would she stay with these people?

She didn't know when she fell asleep, but when she woke—with a start—the room was bathed in black. She panicked. She should have been outside, helping with the food. Once, on Wofa Sarpong's farm, she took a nap and slept past dinnertime. His first wife called her lazy and made her search for firewood with no help from the other girls for a month.

Outside, three children about Hassana's age played with small empty tins. Mma sat on a stool beside a tiny woman, who Aminah found out was Wurche's aunt. They didn't mention anything about Aminah oversleeping. Instead, Mma gave her a huge calabash and asked her to fetch water. She pointed in the direction of Sulemana's room. Aminah didn't understand how a water hole would be in there, but when she got closer, she came to a well surrounded by a ring of large stones, next to which was a small bowl for fetching. She filled the calabash and returned it to Mma, who poured it onto large cuts of meat. Everything suggested that these were wealthy people. Water right there in the courtyard, horses, enormous chunks of meat. Mma passed Aminah a bowl of onions, and she looked approving as she sliced through the first. Aminah was so proud, then, that Na had taught her well. This was sudden: her need to impress. She had spent the last two years not caring.

Mma scooped a handful of shea butter into a pot, which she placed and adjusted on a three-mounded hearth. It was just like at home in Botu. Three small hills fused with the earth.

Wurche came out of her room, balancing the baby on her hip. Now that he was awake, he looked half her size. Aminah had never seen such a huge baby. Wurche handed him to Mma. Aminah was almost done laying out the raffia mats for dinner when a man stepped out of the hut closest to the entrance. He was tall, wearing an elaborate smock with a piece of cloth folded on his shoulder. He had to be Wurche's father. Their faces had the same round shape. Immediately, Aminah curtsied like they did for older men in Botu.

The man said something in the language of Salaga, his voice booming. Then gestured for Aminah to get up.

"She's the girl taking care of Wumpini," said Mma in Hausa. Not long after, Mma whispered with sour, onion-flavored breath, "He's the King of Salaga and Kpembe. I'm sure Wurche didn't tell you, but it's important you know."

Aminah nodded, dumbfounded. The hair on her arms stood up and her skin pocked. No wonder. How had she ended up in the King of Salaga's court?

A large man came out of Wurche's room, trailed by Wurche, and Aminah understood that he was her husband.

When everyone sat down to eat, Mma dished out rice onto three large platters and Aminah poured the meat sauce over the rice, her hand trembling as she felt the King of Salaga's piercing gaze on her. She was nervous because he was king, but also because she was reminded of the man from the caravan, the one whose hand had traveled to places it shouldn't have. And as Aminah tried to focus on the food, the king's gaze never left her. Same with Sulemana. Wurche's husband was the only man not looking at her.

After dinner, Aminah followed Wurche to her room to clean the baby. The room breathed! To get from the floor to the ceiling, would take three people. Chests and baskets large enough to hide a person lined the circular walls of the room, and still there was space. She saw herself in a mirror slanted against the wall next to the window and wished she hadn't looked. Her skin stuck to her bones. Her cornrows had joined in a matted mess, and her eyes were ringed in a darker shade than the rest of her face. Were the men staring at her because she looked sickly? To her, beautiful was Na during pregnancy. In spite of her sadness, Na's skin had looked as smooth as the silt by the water hole, her hair had grown thick, and when she combed it out, one was tempted to sink into its cottony curls. This reflection in the mirror was not beautiful.

The baby gargled as she wiped his plump body with a wet cloth. His father came in and out, and each time, Aminah caught him looking at his wife. She had seen it before, that look. It was the same one that Baba gave Na when she was resolved to win an argument. If it wasn't a look of love, it was certainly admiration. It was too early to begin to understand everyone, but Aminah prayed to Otienu that this house wouldn't have a Wofa Sarpong or, even worse, his son. She was already scared of the king, but she hoped his position required him to be honorable.

"When you get used to him," Wurche said suddenly, "you'll keep him until he falls asleep."

When Wumpini was about eight months old, after Aminah had been at Wurche's for about four months, his father came to her. It was afternoon. Everyone was napping and she was playing outside with Wumpini, who refused to sleep and kept garbling. Adnan crouched before her and stared. He was the last person she expected that from. He usually just smiled, or called out her name as if it were a song, but the only person he had eyes for was his wife. Aminah and Adnan hardly interacted. Steeling herself, she prepared for his proposal. She didn't like the feeling of being sewn up every time she encountered a man—it was exhausting. Would he want the same as Wofa Sarpong? Or more? What about Wurche? Even though she didn't seem to care for Adnan, she would surely kill Aminah if she found out her husband was doing things with her. Wurche was not one of Wofa Sarpong's docile wives.

Adnan reached into a pocket on his smock.

"Do we have milk?" he said.

"I'll go and get some," said Aminah, relieved.

He handed her cowries, then said, "Grind this into a fine powder. Add it to the milk and leave it outside my door, on the left side. Don't tell anyone about it."

He opened up a piece of calico and in it was a gray mass. Aminah had no idea what it was and didn't dare ask what it was for. Happy that his request, strange as it was, had nothing to do with her, she picked up Wumpini, laid his warm body against her back, wrapped a cloth around him and strapped him to her body. She went to the wide spread of green grass where Ahmed the Fulani let his cows graze and sold sour milk. She liked going to buy from Ahmed because his language was close to hers.

She procured the milk, returned home, pounded the unidentifiable object and set it before Wurche and Adnan's room as instructed.

Every ten days or so, Adnan would bring Aminah something to grind and ask her to set it in front of his room. There were dried leaves, rock-like objects, tree barks—almost always things she couldn't identify but which she could easily grind with a smooth rock and slab of stone. Then one day he brought her a dried lizard, preserved in a state of permanent shock.

After getting the milk, she returned to the palace, which was still under the spell of afternoon sleep. She rested the fossilized creature on a big slab of stone, the same one she used to grind onions to pulp. There was no other choice; a man of the house had given her an order. She tried to crush the lizard, but it was as dry and hard as ever. She reached for the mortar, knowing very well she shouldn't pound; it was sure to wake someone, but she couldn't do it at any other time if no one was to see what she was doing. Wurche sometimes yelled at her—*Can't you think?* was her favorite phrase when Aminah, lost in her thoughts, forgot to quench the fire, for instance. For the most part, though, the hospitality she met on the first day was still there, so Aminah had started to grow comfortable. So much so that she did things against her better judgment. Things she would do if she were back in Botu's valleys and fertile soils. Even things she only did when she was in the room she'd shared with Eeyah. She set Wumpini on the mat and gave her back a good stretch, letting out a loud fart.

She dropped the stiff and stony lizard in the mortar's depths and began to feebly pound it, holding in her disgust. She still didn't know what Adnan used his concoctions for. Perhaps a sacrifice? In Botu, the only times dead animals showed up like that was when the boys were playing tricks on the girls or when a sacrifice had to be made, but it was Obado who did the parli. Women were not allowed to touch anything related to the sacrifice. Aminah heard movement. She stopped, looked around. No one emerged. She pounded again a few times.

"Why are you making so much noise?" said Wurche.

Aminah started, then apologized while trying to cook up an excuse. Wurche, not satisfied, edged closer and stood directly over the mortar. While most of the lizard was broken in bits, its ugly head was unground, looking as gnarled as before. Wurche shrieked. Aminah swallowed. Where was Adnan?

"Are you trying to poison us?" Wurche's voice rose.

"Please, Sister," started Aminah.

"Mma, come and see."

Mma shuffled out of her hut, fixing her white veil over her head. She trudged forward, tying her cloth around her chest. She peered into the mortar when Wurche pointed at it.

"Wo yo!" Mma said, covering her mouth.

"Is that what you eat where you're from?" asked Wurche. "You're missing where you come from?"

Aminah shook her head. The lizard, mortar and pestle all grew wavy watery edges. Adnan came out of his room, saw them gathered around the mortar, and left the compound as if it didn't concern him at all.

"Wurche, your father has us grind all sorts of potions for him," said Mma. "This is nothing. I've cooked and ground up a whole monitor lizard into soup to make his men unafraid. Aminah, wash the mortar well when you're done."

Wurche picked up Wumpini and made for her room, wiping his mouth as if Aminah had offered him some of the offending creature. Aminah felt ashamed and wanted to kick the mortar, throw away the whole thing, but she kept pounding. She did this both to maintain her dignity and to release the frustration

Adnan had made her feel. When it was ground to powder, she added it to the bowl of sour milk and set it on the side of the step that led into Wurche's room. When Adnan returned, he would see what a coward he was and feel ashamed for it.

Aminah was about to enter the sweet place just before sleep takes over, that point when you repeat the pleasant images from your day against the silky pink under your eyelids. Her day hadn't been pleasant, but the moment was still sweet. She imagined herself in the green grass where Ahmed's cows grazed, and was about to drift off when Mma came into her room, veil wrapped around her head.

"It wasn't for you, was it?" she said. At first Aminah was disoriented. "The lizard was a man's doing, wasn't it? Look at me. When I say the right name, blink twice."

Mma drew closer and Aminah could feel her breath. Another thing old people had in common: stale breath that whispered that death was close by. "Was it Etuto?"

Aminah did nothing.

"Sulemana?" Her voice had risen in disbelief.

Still, Aminah did nothing. Mma went through a list of Etuto's soldiers. Then she was quiet.

"Ah, Adnan."

Aminah blinked twice.

Mma burst out laughing and mumbled "Wo yo" to herself. "I'm sure you know what it's for," she said.

Aminah shook her head.

"Some say it's for making a love potion. Some say it's for sexual stamina. They say a man with stamina will get his woman to do anything he wants."

He'd been using the potions for weeks, and from the look of things, Wurche was talking less to Adnan and more to Sulemana. It made Aminah feel sorry for Adnan.

"Mma, please don't tell him I told you."

Mma assured Aminah she'd only asked because she was curious. Then she paused, her eyes—gray with age—searching Aminah's, as if looking into her would reveal something. Her voice dropped a notch. "You're a good girl. One can tell these things. Treat us well and you'll be fine here."

Wumpini turned one and his father ordered a large sheep to be slaughtered. The boy still refused to walk so Aminah carried him all morning while frying bowl after bowl of mutton for the guests coming to celebrate the milestone. Two big pots of millet beer sat in the kitchen, acrid vapor rising from them. She couldn't understand why anyone drank such foul-smelling stuff. Skins were spread out before Etuto's and Wurche's huts, and visitors dropped in all morning.

That morning, one of the busiest days Aminah had experienced there so far, Sulemana came over, plucked a piece of meat and asked her where her people were from.

"Botu," said Aminah, but before the conversation went anywhere, a group of men wearing netted talismans, tall riding boots and guns on their shoulders marched in and settled by Etuto's hut. Sulemana joined them, to Aminah's relief. She couldn't carry on a light conversation while focusing on both the food and Wumpini.

Etuto came out and everyone prostrated themselves on the ground before him. This never failed to surprise Aminah. Whether the ground was dusty or muddy, people lay down when they met the Kpembewura. Etuto wore embroidered riding boots, the kind Baba had started making. As if he'd seen her looking at him, Etuto flung his right arm into the air and shouted, "Beer!"

Aminah laid several calabashes on a tray, poured the nauseating liquid into them, and hurried over to Etuto's party. She lowered the tray to Adnan's level. He declined, but thanked her earnestly. Since the lizard incident, the mere sight of his face was enough to annoy Aminah. And then she'd feel bad for being annoyed. It was a curse, the way she easily felt for people.

When she arrived before Etuto, he lifted his calabash and said, "Thank you, to the most beautiful Aminah." His eyes lingered on her face, moved down her chest. Her heart raced. Everyone laughed as if he'd cracked a joke.

More people came in, and Aminah was struck by the sight of two men lingering outside the courtyard, paler than fresh shea butter. They seemed drained of all blood. If Na thought Issa-Na looked uncooked, Aminah was not sure how she would have described these men. So it was a person like that who had bought Husseina at the big water. The new arrivals spoke to Etuto and he commanded his battalion up and out of the compound.

"More beer, Aminah," ordered Etuto.

She went for more calabashes and rushed back to keep up with Etuto. In addition to the pale men was a black man dressed just like them in a shirt and shorts, similar to the inspector who had come to Wofa Sarpong's farm. Etuto led the guests into the compound, where Mma, Wurche, and other Kpembe women were now seated on the skins before Wurche's hut.

The men spoke Gonja, Hausa, and what must have been the pale man's language. Aminah understood from the Hausa that they were there to strengthen some bond they'd already made. And part of that was by offering gifts. The pale men's messengers handed strings of beads to Etuto, who bequeathed them to Wurche. Wurche bowed at the visitors and distributed the beads to Mma and the other women, who burst into ululation. The pale men presented bottles of brown liquid. Ahmed strode in with a black and white cow as tall as the entrance and another man came in with a large sack of yams balanced on his head. Ahmed and the man left and Etuto stood up and pointed to his gifts. If Aminah were the one being presented gifts, she would have been happier with Etuto's offerings.

The men talked for hours, after which the black man dressed like an inspector gave a blue, white and red cloth to Etuto. Later that evening, Mma told Aminah she had just witnessed history being made. By accepting their flag, Etuto had accepted friendship from the British white people. Wurche said the fact that Etuto got up to meet the white people meant that the situation had changed. The white people used to come to him. She said if Etuto had accepted a flag it meant that Salaga was no longer neutral and it was protection, not friendship. Aminah had no clue what they were talking about.

Wurche

While more and more white men penetrated Salaga-Kpembe, each time demanding an audience with Etuto, Wurche's marriage turned into a nightmare. She had to ask Adnan's permission for everything and he took full advantage of his power over her. He forbade her from sitting in on Etuto's meetings, asking what kind of man he would look like if his wife didn't follow the rules. He made her stop teaching with Jaji. If she wanted to go to Salaga, she had to go with him, like a well-behaved married woman. At first she protested, telling him it went against everything she'd learned. She *was* allowed to leave home in pursuit of learning. But he said those were subversive ideas. And when she said she would do as she pleased, he hit her. She tried to tell Etuto, but her father was unraveling. He was so absorbed in keeping Salaga under his control that he insisted she hold off until he was sure no one (the people in Kete-Krachi, the Asante, the French or the Germans) was going to take Salaga. Until then they needed Dagbon's protection. She tried to tell Mma. The old lady, after singing the marriage song for as long as Wurche could remember, suddenly sang a different tune.

"Only after I became a widow did I have peace," said Mma.

Soon, Wurche tried to stop fighting back. Not because she was letting Adnan kill her spirit; it was about self-preservation.

He possessed stores of energy and when she fought back against his increased aggression, she lost. When he busily fondled the nuggets of his prayer beads and stared into space, as he often did, Wurche looked at him, marveling that she'd ever thought him gentle. His face now had all the marks of a violent man. Eyes that had once seemed small and innocent, were shrewd slits. His breathing had always bothered her, but now when he slept it was as if a hungry lion were next to her, taking in deep, ragged breaths, ready to maul her after he was well rested. It was not easy for her to meet his ravenous needs, but she tried.

Instead of fighting back when Adnan hit her, Wurche would wrap Wumpini on her back, pick up an item she valued and move it into Aminah's room. When the sun peeked out on a morning after Adnan had struck her so badly that big blobs of blood bubbled from her nose, she collected two sacks, picked up Wumpini (sleepy and nearly impossible to carry) and walked out. They had fought over where Wumpini slept. Adnan wanted the baby to start sleeping with Aminah or Mma. Wurche knew what that meant—she would be forced to wholly submit to Adnan. She shook her head, refusing to swallow her feelings. Before she could even say the words, Adnan's hand was on her face.

Now, Aminah was up, sweeping. Even in doing a mundane task, the girl's limbs moved elegantly. Wurche watched her, then snapped out of her trance to hand Wumpini and the sacks to her. She returned to her room, where the lion still slept, and wondered, *What if I smothered him?*

"Sister Wurche," floated Aminah's voice. It was too loud. She was enjoying her Adnan-free morning. "Sister, please come see."

In the courtyard, Wumpini was taking tentative steps. He fell down, but immediately got on all fours and pushed himself up to try again. Wurche rushed to him and hugged him. Then terror clutched at her heart.

"Keep the news to yourself," Wurche said.

"But this is good news, Sister," said a confused Aminah.

"Keep carrying him. Don't let anyone see him walk."

Wurche had to buy herself time, as much as she wanted to share the news with Mma and Etuto. But if either of them were told, Adnan would find out too, and they would be off to Dagbon. It was time to do what she hadn't willed herself to do four years before. But first, she had to make sure Aminah was ready.

She asked Aminah to bring Wumpini and a cloth. She saddled and mounted Baki, swaddled the toddler in front with the cloth, and set off, signaling Aminah to follow. They were too close to the palace for her to be seen riding Wurche's horse. Wurche trod down the tree-lined road to Salaga, then turned off a narrow path to the right, stopped the horse, and asked Aminah to climb on. Aminah hesitated and Wurche swore under her breath. Aminah stared and stared. When she decided to act, she put a foot in the right stirrup, but couldn't get the other foot up.

"Give me your right hand," said Wurche.

Aminah did, but still wouldn't lift her left foot.

"Aminah, lift your foot."

"Sorry, Sister."

Aminah stepped aside and Wurche let go of her hand, got off the horse and tied Wumpini on her back. She slotted Aminah's foot back in the stirrup and pushed her bottom till Aminah was high enough to clamber up. Wurche got back on the horse, muttering, "Ay, Allah! *My* life is shortened when a commoner rides a horse, not Baki's."

Wumpini laughed giddily as they bumped down the path. They got to the forest of her childhood, the place where she learned to shoot with Sulemana, where she and Fatima had played, where she'd dreamed wildly. She got down first, helped Aminah off, and tied Baki to a tree. The trees, taller now, were arranged in straight lines—Mma said she and her friends had planted them as girls. She looked up at the canopy of the trees and remembered Fatima's enthusiastic claps whenever Wurche finished a speech. Wurche wondered where her childhood friend had ended up and what she'd have said if she learned that Wurche was no closer to getting the things she wanted.

"At home, always carry him on your back. I don't want to see him walking in the house. Here, he can walk freely," said Wurche, untying Wumpini and letting him slide down her back. As much as she didn't want Adnan to find this out, she also wanted Wumpini to become independent fast. He wobbled, took a step and fell. Wurche clapped. The boy got up again and took more steps. She pointed to a tree a short distance away, about ten steps for Wumpini. "Aminah, go there. Yes, Wumpini, go to Aminah."

As Wumpini wobbled over, Wurche watched Aminah. Her cheeks had filled out and she wore her hair neatly braided. Wurche understood why all the men were enamored with her. Aminah. She had lived with them for over a year and kept to herself; she did her work, didn't complain. Moro's girl. Every single man in the house was entranced by her, so she had no doubt that Moro, too, was bewitched. It wasn't just Aminah's arresting physical appearance, but something quiet and rested in the girl, which had attracted Wurche, too. Hers wasn't Wurche's lost and restless energy, it wasn't Mma's worrisome nature, Sulemana's earnestness, nor Etuto's covetousness. One wanted to keep staring at her. Or become her. Or devour her. Wurche shoved these thoughts out of her head. She needed to stay focused.

For a week, Wurche made Aminah pack the items she'd stored in her room into sacks, and the three of them took trips into the forest to allow Wumpini to walk and for Aminah to get used to Baki. They might be traveling soon, she told Aminah, so she had to learn to mount Baki with speed.

Two days later, Etuto summoned Wurche to his quarters. He looked swollen. The skin under his eyes sagged with the lack of sleep, and his lips were bloated with alcohol.

"Those Kete-Krachi princes must be dealt with," he slurred. "I'm sending Sulemana to the Gold Coast because those princes want to destroy Salaga."

Now that he was friends with the British, he wanted them to help him take military action. The Kete-Krachi people had even begun to poach his best soldiers. He sucked from his wineskin.

"Will you go with them? Having a woman in the delegation might soften the governor's heart."

"Yes." She didn't pause to consider her husband or her son or her plan to escape. This was the start of what she really wanted.

"They leave tomorrow," said Etuto. "At dawn."

She went into Aminah's room, thankful she'd already put aside some of her belongings. Aminah was curled around Wumpini's portly form.

"I'm going to the Gold Coast tomorrow," Wurche whispered. "Pick out three of my best smocks ..."

Just then Mma poked her head in.

"Aminah, go and get sour milk from the Fulani boy for Sulemana's voyage."

"I'm going with him," said Wurche.

"And your husband?" asked Mma.

Wurche shrugged, then turned to Aminah. "Pack when you come back."

Aminah looked nervously at Wumpini, whose heavy breathing was now a series of snores. It was fine. Aminah could go and come back and the child would still be asleep. All three women left the hut. Wurche went into hers and found Adnan propped up in bed, his prayer beads looped in his right hand. She said nothing to him. She would need her gun for the trip, she would need a hat, and—this would surely please Mma—she would need her kohl. If a bit of charm and seduction was needed to convince the governor, so be it. As she riffled through her basket of combs and the jewelry she never wore, she heard a shriek. She rushed outside. Adnan followed. Etuto came out of his hut. Mma was clapping into the air and shouting. At her shins, Wumpini walked as if he'd been born doing it.

"Ay, Allah!" shouted Mma.

Wurche didn't know whether to feign indifference or act surprised. In walked Aminah with two small pots. She paused, made eye contact with Wurche.

"Yes! Thank Allah!" shouted Wurche, rushing to pick up Wumpini.

"I thought this day would never come," said Adnan. "Finally, we can go home. Etuto, my dear father, with your permission, we would like to head to Dagbon as soon as possible and give you your space."

"And my journey tomorrow?" said Wurche, with Wumpini struggling to get down. She fixed her gaze on her father. His smock seemed to swallow him. She'd never seen him look so small. No one said a thing. Even the leaves stood still. "Etuto?"

"If your husband gives you permission," he said.

Wurche, who didn't want to give Adnan the satisfaction of telling her what to do, beckoned Aminah, and walked towards her room.

"Prepare the sacks I gave you, and put all your belongings into a sack or bag. Carry them outside. Then take Baki and tie her loosely to the tree outside. Put the sacks astride her and wait for me. Here."

She strapped Wumpini to Aminah's back, took a long, deep breath and went into her room. She picked up the gun Dramani had given her and looked about the room. She didn't have time to go through the rest of her things. If Adnan was smart and saw Aminah carrying bags, he would start drawing conclusions. She left the room and saw Baki's rump disappear through the entrance. Good. Aminah was almost ready. Adnan was the only one in the courtyard.

"Adnan," Wurche said, walking towards him while holding the gun's barrel. Adnan might think she was going to use it on him, but the smug expression on his face—the corners of his mouth tilted up and his nose snout-like—suggested it was the last thing on his mind.

"After we got married, I lay with another man," she said, standing before him.

Silence. Adnan's expression softened. He dropped his prayer beads and Wurche took it as her chance to flee. She told Aminah to run as she untied Baki. Aminah bolted, Wumpini bouncing up and down on her back, and Wurche followed, dragging Baki's reins. The sacks made Baki sluggish, but she soon got off to a trot.

"Whore! Sheitan!" Adnan bellowed.

Wurche felt her pulse even in her ears. She and Aminah and Baki ran. Wurche looked back and was relieved but slightly disappointed when she found no one in pursuit. They got on the path that led to the forest and mounted Baki. Their destination: Kete-Krachi.

They passed through three towns before Wurche was confident that they were far enough from Kpembe to stop. They bought milk and maasa from a girl carrying a crown of a basket on her head, then continued the journey, stopping another three towns later to clean Wumpini and rest Baki. It seemed like Kete-Krachi would never come. After a day of traveling with pauses for food and rest, a man in Hiamankyen assured them Kete-Krachi was next.

As they entered the town, Wurche heard the sound of water lapping against a shore: a slap followed by a receding whisper, at once violent and soothing. She wondered how long it would take her to grow used to this place's secrets, its nighttime smell, the sound of its dawn. The grass was dry and patchy, but the air was damp and her skin didn't feel as taut as it did in Salaga. Several huts, some rectangular, some round, lined the road leading into the town. She'd planned her escape, but hadn't planned how long she'd stay away. A man crossed the road into the town, a hoe slung over his left shoulder. Wurche greeted him in Gonja, but he returned a blank stare and only when she spoke in Hausa did he return a curt nod. When she mentioned Jaji, he shook his head.

"No horses," he said instead.

"Why?" said Wurche.

"Dente doesn't allow horses."

Wurche sighed and dismounted. She shouldn't get on the bad side of the powerful oracle of Dente on the first day in his town. She took Wumpini from Aminah, who scrambled down ungracefully. Wurche set Wumpini down, untied the sacks, handed two to Aminah and took the last. She tethered Baki to a tree with a complex knot and pressed her forehead to the horse's crest.

Even if her relief was mixed with regret, Wurche felt a sudden desire to laugh. All these years, she'd felt caved in, imprisoned, and suddenly, finally, she'd broken free. She felt as if she were floating on air. She would miss her family, but none of them had said, *Adnan is no good, here's your way out.*

They were strolling, but the town was only now waking up, so Wurche wasn't worried. If they didn't find someone who knew Jaji, they would go to the mosque. The local imam was sure to know her or her imam. A group of thin girls wisped by carrying empty pots. Wurche greeted them and described what Jaji looked like (tall, always in a straw hat when she was out) and two of the girls pointed to a rectangular house behind a set of round ones. Wurche asked them if Aminah could follow them to fetch water for Baki.

After Aminah watered Baki, they went to Jaji, who answered her door when they announced themselves and gasped with surprise.

"I've done a terrible thing," said Wurche.

"What?"

"I've run away from my marriage."

"Ay, Allah."

Jaji offered them seats and asked them to sit while she got water. Then she wanted to be told all. Wurche, not wanting to appear small before Aminah, spoke in Gonja. She told Jaji she'd had enough of Adnan's violence and that she ran away before he could take them to Dagbon, that if she stayed she would never get to do anything useful or any activity she enjoyed. Jaji said her accommodation was modest, but she was always happy to have Wurche's help.

"What should I do about my horse? A man said I couldn't bring her in because of the Dente."

"Horses are fine in Kete," said Jaji. "It used to be that in Krachi the Dente forbade horses. But he was executed last year. I don't know if it means horses are now allowed there. I'm never really in Krachi ..."

"He was executed?" said Wurche. She should have heard about it. Then again, Adnan had made sure she was shielded from all things political. And Moro, who would have told her, was long gone from her life. She wondered how long it would take before they saw each other again.

"The Germans shot him. They want to control the people and the people were only listening to the Dente. Before he was killed, people near and far were frightened of him. For a long time, he didn't allow traders in Kete-Krachi. It was only after signing an agreement with the British that Kete became a market town. In fact, some people here think the reason the Germans shot the Dente is because he was friends with the British. Welcome to a new set of politics. I thought I was escaping Salaga ... but I digress. The rules are more relaxed here than in Krachi. Go get your horse. You can keep it here. The person was mistaken."

Wurche sent Aminah for Baki. Jaji's room was smaller than any of the rooms in Kpembe. It was too small for four people, including one who had just discovered his legs. Wurche would have to search for other accommodation.

Aminah was gone for over an hour. When she returned her forehead was crumpled in sweat, confusion, and fear.

"The horse wasn't there, Sister," she said. She had searched everywhere. Even up and down the river.

Jaji sucked her teeth. "Theft has become the order of the day here."

"I've had that horse since I was ten." There had to be some mistake. She slid to the floor. She needed to feel grounded. "Are you sure you looked everywhere?"

"Yes, Sister."

Wurche stood up, stepped out of Jaji's hut. Aminah was not one for lying. She looked to the right: a laterite path lined with huts on either side of it. To the left: another red path with dawadawa trees. Ahead, the river raced by, brown and indifferent. She walked to the tree where she'd left Baki. No Baki. She went back to Jaji's. Losing Baki was not part of her plan.

"She's so unique; if the thief lives anywhere in Kete-Krachi, he'll be caught," said Jaji.

Wurche sank to the ground again. The loss of Baki made the move feel like a mistake. She stared at the pile of yellowing paper next to Jaji's bed.

Aminah

Not long after their arrival in Kete-Krachi, Jaji announced she was expecting visitors, one of whom was not Wurche's favorite person, but he'd been good to Jaji, so if Wurche didn't want to see him, she was welcome to disappear for a few hours. Wurche stayed, sat on a mat, and didn't get up when they walked in. Only she could get away with being rude to guests, and men, at that, Aminah thought.

When the guests arrived, she also recognized someone—the man who was supposed to buy her! He stared at her as if they knew each other, forcing her to look away. Of all the emotions going through her, the strongest was shame, which she couldn't explain since she had done nothing wrong. The second man—Jaji called him Shaibu—was dressed in an ornate blue-and-white smock that kissed his ankles. The third was a pale man in a black uniform with a black belt and gold buttons, clutching a rigid hat. Aminah had seen pale men when they visited Etuto in Kpembe, but this was the first time she could stay close enough to study one. He had all the parts that a regular person possessed—eyes, nose, mouth, ears—and his limbs were similar to everyone else's, but the browns of his eyes were green and almost glasslike. When he greeted in Hausa, his words were jerky and halting, and Aminah had to hold in her laughter. At first, Wurche stood stiffly by Jaji. Then Shaibu stuck out his hand and said something that caused her to crack a smile and shake his outstretched hand. She said something back to him in Gonja.

"Wurche, the lovely princess of Kpembe," said Shaibu to the men, in Hausa. "I told her she's rejected my advances since we were boy and girl, so I've come to accept that we are brother and sister, that we shouldn't let our fathers' sins affect our friendship. I am a peaceful man and I have no grievance against her."

"And *I* told him he tried to kill my father," said Wurche, back straight. She seemed to be enjoying the banter. Wurche thrived on conflict, or just being different from everybody else, it appeared. "You backed Nafu, so we're enemies. And if you want us to be friends, you'll find my horse and deal with the thief appropriately."

"Wurche, we both know I am a coward," said Shaibu. "My life comes first. The day I follow a group on a suicide mission, the sun won't rise. I made sure to leave for Kete-Krachi as soon as that war began. Jaji told me about your horse. Someone stole one of my finest smocks my first week here. We'll keep looking for it. Now, let me introduce my friends." He gestured at the man who'd bought Aminah. "I believe you already know Moro." Then he flung his hand in the direction of the white man. "And this is Helmut."

Wurche regarded Moro and smiled strangely. It was a pout, with eyes that flirted and said Wurche knew some secret of his. Moro smiled back curtly.

Shaibu said when he heard that Wurche had moved to Kete-Krachi, they had to come pay their respects. "Moro made me, really. But it would have been impolite of us to ignore the wild princess of Kpembe, so here we are."

They couldn't stay for lunch, which was a relief, because Aminah had only made enough for four.

"Find my horse," shouted Wurche, as they left.

*

When Aminah found out Baki had been stolen, she walked the entire way back to Jaji's house as if clay had hardened around her feet. When she saw the way Wurche crumpled to the floor, she grew irritated, but she understood. Baki was like family to Wurche. For a week, Wurche couldn't be consoled; she even wore brown mourning clothes. Jaji told her she could buy a new horse from the stables, but she wouldn't budge. She said a horse couldn't be replaced just like that. Aminah was sure Baki was lost simply because Wurche was too proud to ask for help. She'd told Shaibu to find the horse, but he didn't seem the kind of man to involve himself in any kind of labor. Wurche could have gone to the stables herself to find out if someone had tried to sell a horse that looked like Baki; instead she wore mourning clothes. A small part of Aminah was happy the horse was stolen, because it meant one less task to worry about. She wouldn't have to wake up before the sun rose to clean the creature. She hated that, just after she had wiped it, it would let out a long stream of urine that always, always splashed on her.

After that first visit, the three men would not stop coming to Jaji's house. Every time they came, Shaibu ate, Helmut tickled Wumpini till he was in stitches and Moro watched Aminah. At first she concluded that he thought she had betrayed him by going with Wurche. But when his gaze continued to burn into her, her shame shifted into a small flutter, the tremor of a butterfly's wings, and it became curious about him and began to return his stares.

One afternoon, Wurche's fingers grazed the bottom hump of Moro's upper arm and pinched his flesh as if she were owner of his body, the way one would hold a bag. She whispered in his ear, and whatever it was molded a frown on his forehead, making Aminah feel strange. Jealous. Just then he shifted his gaze to her and his scrunched lips stretched into a smile. She went outside. While she was washing the platter they had eaten on, he followed.

"Is Wurche treating you well?"

Her heart almost stopped beating. Words refused to leave her mouth, so she nodded and looked down at her washing.

Another afternoon, she prepared a delicious pot of rice and beans because she knew he would be coming to Jaji's. She took her time, removed all the stones from the beans and washed the rice three times. The last time she had folded any love into a meal she prepared was in Botu. This time, she went to the market early, chose the best ginger and garlic, plucked the ripest tomatoes from Jaji's garden. At the butcher's she batted her eyes and asked for the softest cuts of mutton. So when only Shaibu and Helmut showed up she couldn't hide her disappointment. Everybody thought she was sick. Jaji even insisted Aminah lie down. Her body felt pulled by the ground and it was hard to lift herself off the mat.

Later, when the room was quiet, Wumpini asleep by her side, Jaji and Wurche away, she realized she wasn't thinking clearly. She was being foolish. This was a man who had tried to buy her, one who could be worse than of any of the others she had encountered so far. His physical appearance was distracting her. He was no different from the horsemen.

He had taken Khadija to Salaga. He was beautiful to behold; that much no one could deny. But beauty was so personal, Aminah thought. Her twin sisters, for instance—two people who shared the same dreams—had different ideas about beauty. To Hassana, their neighbor Motaaba was the ugliest boy in Botu. Aminah and Husseina didn't agree, although adolescence had robbed him of beauty. What was it that made one person attractive to many people? Power? The madugu of the caravans was someone everyone thought handsome. Moro didn't have half the madugu's power, and yet she and Wurche were both attracted to him. She had to keep reminding herself of who he was.

*

They stayed with Jaji for three long months and tried to keep out of her way—Aminah took Wumpini for walks along the river and Wurche disappeared, but even the saintly Jaji had bad days. One morning, Aminah woke up early and stole the chance to bathe on her own before Wumpini woke up. Even with the twins Aminah had never felt so starved of time. It felt as if every minute awake was spent with Wumpini. So as she bathed she took her time, scrubbed every part of her body, and when she was done she felt good about life, a feeling that ended when she heard Wumpini's piercing bawl. When she got to the hut, the stink of toilet hit her. Wumpini had relieved himself on a piece of paper on the floor. He was screaming in the corner and Jaji stood off to the side arms folded, her face expressionless.

"I am sorry, Jaji," said Aminah. "What should I do about your work?"

"It's fine. It's just a newspaper."

Aminah rushed to get a rag, soapy water and sand. It was clear Jaji had had enough of them. Aminah wondered if it meant they would soon return to Salaga—Wurche hadn't said anything about how long they would stay, and Aminah was sure Jaji wanted to know. Aminah struck a match and lit a pot of incense, then took Wumpini outside for his wash. He kept hiccuping as she wiped his tears. His resemblance to Adnan was uncanny.

The incident must have pushed Wurche to act, because not long after, Shaibu brought news that they could build a home behind Jaji's. The Germans had authorized it. It suggested permanence. And Aminah found she was glad. As much as she had liked the people in Kpembe, she had more freedom in Kete-Krachi. It didn't take long to clean Jaji's hut, so she spent many mornings walking along the river with Wumpini, her mind wandering. She was so pleased with the news that when Moro offered to build the huts, she said she would help him. She couldn't tell what spirit had possessed her to be so bold.

"Speaking of Germans," said Wurche, after Shaibu's announcement, "where's Helmut?"

"He's gone to Salaga, then he'll continue on to Dagbon," said Shaibu. "They have to clear up a problem. It sounds like the British have breached the agreement they signed with your father and the Germans." He craned his head forward, wet his lips as though he were about to eat a tasty dish, and said, "He seems to have taken a shine to you."

Wurche ignored him and asked when the building would begin. Moro was ready to begin the next day.

He showed up as the muezzin's second call to prayer was rising to a long, loud wail. Wurche came out of Jaji's hut and greeted him coolly. Aminah tried to understand their relationship. Moro would smile at Wurche, she would respond as if she didn't care, then she would try to touch him and he would stiffen up.

Moro brought sacks of wattle and a straight stick and told Aminah to stand in the middle of what would become the first hut. He handed her one end of the stick, angled the other end and used it to trace a circle in the earth. Wurche instructed that the door face the sun. She was like a hawk, watching every move Moro and Aminah made. It was only when Wumpini woke up and came outside that Wurche left Moro and Aminah alone, but before she did, she trained her eyes on Aminah, as if she could tell the emotions coursing through her.

Moro dug a foundation in the circle, Wumpini played nearby atop a pile of sand, and Aminah went down to the river to fetch a pot of water. She missed Kpembe's wells and how they were right in the middle of the compound. Droves of cattle dragged carts of salt along the riverbank and canoes glided up and down the river. In one canoe were about ten people—mostly girls, with metal ringed around their necks. Aminah shuddered, wondering where they would end up. Aminah wasn't free either, but she was no longer faced with the uncertainty that they were. She watched them until they became one with the horizon.

On the second day, as she was pouring water into a small hole Moro had dug in a mixture of sand and wattle, he touched her hand. His mud-caked palm rested just above her wrist and she felt a surge of energy run up her arms. He seemed on the verge of saying something but held back. He took his hand away. Excitement and fear mixed together in her body. He's a slave raider, Aminah reminded herself. Just then, Wurche came out of her hut.

On the third day, Moro said, "I am glad things happened the way they did." Aminah didn't look at him, unsure if she was allowed to have this conversation. "It means we can be friends."

She studied the block she was placing on the wall, her heart pumping wildly. As Wurche's property, did she have the right to a friend? At Wofa Sarpong's they were so isolated from other people that the question had never come up. She forced herself to think of Moro's evil side. The people in the canoes flitted into her mind. She didn't want a friend like Moro.

Aminah missed the simple beauty of Botu. Apart from its trees and gentle hills and the water hole, their huts were colorful and covered with beautiful shapes and lines. In Kpembe and Kete-Krachi, the huts were white and black or just mud-colored. When they finished the huts, Aminah traced three lines around her hut's door and drew waves between the lines. Wurche said nothing. Working on the huts reminded Aminah that she liked working with her hands. If Wurche ever let her go, if she won her freedom, she would want to make things. Clothes or pots. Or shoes.

Na used to tell her to speak her troubles, not hold them in, although neither of them had practiced this often enough. She hadn't found a sympathetic, disinterested ear for a while, but something in the way Jaji talked to Wurche—with a hint of respect, even though she was the teacher—something in her eyes, told Aminah she could trust the teacher with her problems. When Wumpini napped, Aminah went to her. She was seated on a mat, clutching large sheets of paper. Aminah stood by the wall, cleared her throat, and knelt down. Jaji's brows rose to kiss the edge of her white veil, and Aminah burst into tears.

"Oh dear girl, what's wrong?" said Jaji reaching forward and taking Aminah's hand.

Aminah sniffled, searching for words. "I am nineteen," she began and then couldn't stop. She told Jaji about Baba's disappearance, about being snatched by the horsemen, losing her brother and sisters, staying in a forest and ending up in the Salaga market. Tears had blurred her vision and Jaji wiped them with the hem of her veil.

"Will I ever know freedom again?" asked Aminah.

Jaji sighed. "I'll tell you what I've been hearing." She looked above Aminah's head, towards the door, and lowered her voice. "The chiefs here, in Salaga, and all over the place, really, have been signing treaties with the English and the Germans. What most of them don't know is that the treaties are calling for an end to slavery. One of my own teachers, Alhaji Umar—you have seen him around the mosque, white hair and white beard, Salaga's old imam—he used to say the chiefs should resist the English and the Germans. He calls them Christians. But last time I talked to him, he said he understood why the chiefs were signing treaties; their arms were toys compared to the weapons of the Christians. The mighty Asante, for instance, have already been defeated a few times. You look lost. I hope I'm not confusing you."

"No, Jaji," said Aminah, wondering when the teacher would make her point.

"Good. He said the Christians have some good ideas. They are bringing all sorts of improvements, like more schools, wide roads, more security. And they are calling for an end to slavery. Alhaji Umar said the Christians, like us Muslims, took part in slavery for centuries, they encouraged the slave raids that the likes of Babatu and our friend Moro specialize in, and suddenly they want it to end. In the Gold Coast, which is where this newspaper came from—I'm learning English, you see—slavery has been banned. Just over the river, imagine. It's called emancipation."

Aminah didn't realize how much Jaji talked, and began to regret sharing her story, especially since Jaji's solutions mattered across the river, not here. Her solutions meant Aminah should have stayed with Wofa Sarpong.

And as if the teacher had heard Aminah's thoughts, she added, "All this is to say, it's only a matter of time before it comes this way, and I personally will be glad when that happens. My advice is to bide your time. Wurche will understand when the time comes. She has a kind heart."

Aminah was about to thank Jaji for her time to prevent her from going on, when the rushed patter of running feet broke the conversation. Outside, a short distance away, a large crowd had gathered in a circle. Their blended voices were loud, rough, incomprehensible, yet somehow they managed to move as a unit. Jaji grabbed her straw hat and went with them. Aminah followed, praying Wumpini would continue sleeping for a while. Jaji tapped the shoulder of a woman on the outside of the throng and asked what was happening.

"He's a thief!" said the woman, spit flying from her mouth, her eyes bulging wildly. But she couldn't say what he'd stolen. Realizing she hadn't given any useful information she said, "He was being beaten and asked to be taken to the German barracks."

Jaji nodded and backed away from the crowd. Aminah wanted to follow them to find out if he was the man who had stolen Baki. She pushed herself into the crowd, became one with it. These were things she used to do in Botu. If Wurche asked where she'd gone, she would pretend that she thought Jaji had done the same. She pushed until she was in the middle of the crowd, which allowed her peeks of the person being dragged along. His semi-naked body was covered with welts, his face swollen. He couldn't walk, so two men had propped him up by the armpits. Some people shouted for him to be beaten more and others asked that everyone stay patient, wait for the Germans. Aminah could barely see where they were going. She was carried along with the crowd's thrust, so when they stopped, she almost fell.

The whitewashed German barracks, the largest buildings in Kete-Krachi, were bordered black on the bottom, their gardens adorned with whitewashed rocks. They had stopped in front of the smallest building, and from it came a thin white man in the same kind of uniform Helmut wore. Another white man came out, then another, till there were six of them carrying heavy-looking arms.

The one who seemed to be the highest in command pointed his gun at the crowd, causing it to part. The two men who'd been carrying the accused stepped forward and dumped him in the dirt.

"He stole a cow," said the man on the right, wiping his bloodied hands on his smock.

"What does your imam say?" asked the white man in halting Hausa.

"The thief insisted that we bring him to you," responded the man with the bloodied smock.

The white men conferred with each other. One of them went over to the accused and studied him.

"Take him to your imam," said the leader of the white men. "And stop beating him."

The crowd groaned and the two men collected the beaten man, as one would pick up a lifeless object. Aminah separated herself from them and ran back to the house, almost fainting from fright when she arrived. Wurche was carrying Wumpini, a tear on his round cheek, the back of his plump hand in his mouth. Aminah narrated the whole affair, but Wurche wasn't satisfied. She swiped a slap across Aminah's face. The first time she'd done that. For some reason, Aminah guessed it wasn't really about her leaving Wumpini alone.

Wumpini squirmed out of his mother's grip and stretched out his pudgy arms for Aminah. Wurche drew him closer to her chest and carried him to her hut. Aminah's ears still rang from the slap. Once, in Salaga, Aminah overheard someone say the only way a slave could be free was if his or her master died. She didn't have it in her to kill Wurche or anyone, but now she thought it would be easier if Wurche died of a terrible illness. Then, just as quickly, she felt bad for nursing the thought.

Aminah entered Jaji's room with a tray of boiled yam and bitter-leaf stew. The usual guests were gathered. Jaji had burned incense and the scent had filled the room. Moro took the tray from Aminah as if he were relieving her of a heavy load. Meanwhile, Wurche was telling the group that she wanted to raise animals.

"I'll start with chickens. Aminah will do the building. She finished our house with the nicest designs."

Aminah thought Wurche hadn't noticed the designs.

"I'll help her," said Moro.

Aminah wanted to see Wurche's reaction, but she couldn't look at the woman's face. No one's, really. She felt naked. She felt everyone's eyes on her. She shifted her gaze to Helmut, the other outsider in the group. His boyish face reddened from the pepper as he ate. He was oblivious to the tension Aminah felt. She wondered what made him different from his brothers, those who held guns at the crowd when they'd brought in a criminal, treating them as if *they* were the criminals. Why, wondered Aminah, was Helmut always at Jaji's or with Shaibu and Moro? No other white men associated so closely with them. He wiped his wet nose with the back of his palm. Her thoughts drifted back to Moro. If he was as kind as he seemed to be—constantly offering to help—why did he raid villages, split up families, sell people? These questions scratched at her insides and prevented her from even trying to be friends with him.

"The Salagawura is throwing a naming ceremony for his son," said Shaibu. He turned to Wurche. "Will you come?"

"Doesn't it sound ridiculous to you, naming a person who lives outside Salaga 'Salagawura'? It's disrespectful and senseless," said Wurche.

Aminah still didn't understand much about local politics, but she knew Wurche had betrayed her father by coming to Kete-Krachi, a fact she made up for by always vehemently defending him. The people who fled to Kete-Krachi after some big battle in Salaga had elected a new chief, the Salagawura, as the head of the Salaga immigrants, but Wurche called him illegitimate, useless.

"There is only one chief of Salaga," continued Wurche, "and he's the Kpembewura." She turned to Helmut and said, "Your people caused this."

"I just take orders," said Helmut, sniffling.

Wurche said she wasn't going to the ceremony and stomped out, calling Aminah and Moro outside. She stopped next to Aminah's hut.

"I've decided. I'll raise chickens."

Chickens reeked, so Aminah was not thrilled at having a coop for a neighbor.

Wurche pressed her palm to Moro's arm and raised the other hand to shoulder height. "Just this high. Aminah, stand there and stretch out your hands." She stretched hers too, and their fingertips touched. Wurche pressed into Aminah's hands and stared at her with a look that confused Aminah. A cross between desire and admonishment. Then just as suddenly, Wurche let go and went to Moro. She squeezed his arm and led him back into Jaji's hut.

That night, Aminah couldn't sleep. Anger had filled her chest. Wurche's touching game and Moro's coolness. Moro and everything he stood for. It was good she was angry. When with Wofa Sarpong, she was squeezed of all feeling, which was probably why she did nothing for so long. Anger was good. Anger motivated her. Anger made her bite Kwesi's nose. Who knew where anger would lead this time?

The next day, Moro showed up before Aminah had even bathed. She wiped the crusty corners of her mouth and passed her palms over her eyes. Her hair was untidy, but there was nothing she could do.

He'd brought strips of dried palm leaves that they wove into mats and eventually hoisted up and supported with sticks. They finished the chicken enclosure with a door. Aminah opened and closed the door, amazed at how beautiful it looked. Moro came to her side. Then he placed his palm over her hand on the door. She snatched her hand away.

His gentle expression was briefly replaced with confusion. He broke his gaze, looked off to the side, then stared at Aminah.

"I wish you didn't kidnap and sell people," said Aminah, before she could stop herself. Saying those words made her bolder. "Why did you want to buy me? To make me your slave?"

"No. Not to make you my slave. When I saw you in front of Maigida's, it felt like I'd been searching for you without knowing I'd been searching. It felt as if every horrible thing I'd done in my past was so I could find you." He paused, then said, "I'm sorry for everything you have suffered."

In Botu, Eeyah often talked about "licabili." Aminah had never given it much thought. It was the belief that whatever path you took in life, it would take you where it was supposed to take you. It hadn't been as important to her because things had been the same for the first fifteen years of her life. She knew Botu so well and had no reason to leave it, so it had never seemed like life would take her somewhere else. Did it mean that everything she had been through—losing her family, the horsemen, Wofa Sarpong—had led her to this man? Her palms sweated. She used to think that Otienu could control the things that happened to you if you appeased him or if you were good, but who Otienu was or where he dwelled, she couldn't even say. Eeyah used to say Otienu was everywhere, but now she wasn't sure. Maybe things occurred just because and there was no why. They stared at each other, and he smiled. Aminah willed herself not to smile back. She was too confused.

Wurche stepped out of her hut. She opened and closed the new door, marveling just as Aminah had earlier. "Wonderful work. Let's not waste a single moment. Aminah, feed Wumpini and then go get the chickens from the market."

Wurche

When she'd first seen Moro, she'd been hopeful that, with Adnan out of the way, they could rekindle their romance. And when he flinched every time she tried to touch him in the places he liked, she decided to be bolder. She began to touch him around Aminah—because anybody with eyes could sense what was brewing between them—but he would pry her fingers away. Once, through gritted teeth, he'd warned her to stop. That evening, when only he and Shaibu had showed up at Jaji's, they'd had a conversation about Aminah.

"I want her back," he'd whispered.

"I paid for her," said Wurche.

"She was not yours to pay for. I'll buy her back from you, then."

"She's not for sale. And if you carry on like this, she will be. But I'll sell her to someone going south on the river."

With that last statement, Wurche had unleashed on him all her buried frustrations, her rage, her confusion—a flood of emotions that annoyed her. She wasn't proud of having bought Aminah, especially at a time when she'd been wrestling with the concept of owning people. Nor was she proud of threatening to send Aminah south. But mostly, she was unsettled by the sudden thought of life without Aminah. Aminah anchored her. For one, the girl took Wumpini off her hands. But also, when Aminah was around, she felt safety and peace and something more she wanted to keep buried. This something more appeared in her dreams, with Aminah slowly taking the place of her friend Fatima. In waking life, though, Wurche was sure Aminah would never be as willing as Fatima had been.

But Wurche kept such thoughts and feelings at bay. She had plenty to keep her busy—more pressing matters than dreams that couldn't come alive. She liked her independence in Kete-Krachi, but she also missed Kpembe. She missed having a horse and the space to ride it. She missed her family. She missed the politics of Kpembe. In order to go back to Kpembe and truly thrive there, she needed to stay independent. It meant having money. Now that she had a new business, she would start saving. When she made enough money from the chickens, she would start buying horses. It was more lucrative. Money also meant power. Staying independent meant having information. She taught the women of Kete-Krachi with Jaji during the day and spent evenings studying Jaji's manuscripts when Shaibu, Moro and Helmut weren't around. When they showed up, she pressed them for political developments in Kete-Krachi and beyond. She learned that the Germans had recruited a large number of Hausa men for their army, that the British were also moving farther up the region, even as far up as Dagbon, to sign treaties with the chiefs. The Germans were not happy about this. But, again, she only got flashes of information, because the men only wanted to be regaled by Aminah's food and Shaibu changed the subject whenever she tried to get more details.

One evening, she followed Shaibu and Helmut to the German barracks. She hoped that by spending more time with them she would learn about the European strategy. Her thinking was that if she found enough intelligence on the Germans,

Etuto would forgive her when she returned to Kpembe. More importantly, she would become the person to deal with the white men because she understood them. She would be able to tell if they were helping or hurting her people.

A full blue moon hung low in the sky, casting a clear path. The river shimmered in the moonlight, calm and glassy, until a canoe rowed by. At the barracks, two seated guards leapt up, saluted Helmut, and said nothing as Wurche and Shaibu trailed him. Helmut led them up a veranda and into a main hall.

The room contained twelve wooden chairs arranged in three rows, facing a desk with another wooden chair. In Kpembe meetings were arranged in circles. A black, white and red flag was stuck in a pot next to the desk in front. Helmut herded them through a doorway to the right of the desk. A small lamp was stuck in the wall, a miserable wisp of black smoke wafting up from the tip of the fire. The lit hallway was lined with doors on either side. Helmut led them into his room. In it was a wooden bed laid with a white sheet and pillow; a desk with three piles of books; and two chairs next to the desk. Shaibu made for a large wooden contraption. He sat before it and flipped up its cover, revealing a row of ivory and black rectangles that he pounded on with all his being.

Wurche sat on the bed, frightened, as Shaibu released cacophonous discord from the instrument. After she'd overcome her fright, she went closer and tried to figure out what Shaibu thought he was doing. Helmut shoved Shaibu off the seat, and played a beautiful somber tune. Shaibu nodded, stuck his hands in the air as if he were holding an imaginary stick, and bobbed his head. White people were strange, and Shaibu was being sucked into their world.

"What is this?" said Wurche.

"A piano," said Shaibu.

"Bach, a German composer, says there's nothing remarkable about playing it. And he may be right," said Helmut. "It was also cumbersome to ship, but it keeps me from being homesick."

He opened a large chest and riffled through it. He held out a green bottle and three clear glasses—the same kind Mma kept in her treasure chest of gifts she'd received from the Europeans—and set them on the table. He poured out liquid as clear as water and passed the glasses to his guests. Wurche held hers, small and smooth, sniffed its contents and almost passed out. It smelled even stronger than the stuff her father liked. Shaibu, still annoying Wurche, suggested she drink it in one go. She did as he said and poured the drink into her mouth, swallowing it in one gulp. The liquid burned her throat, choking her. Helmut downed his and patted her back. She found nothing pleasurable in it and pulled a face.

"It's what comes after that's wonderful," said Helmut.

Her insides warmed. She took another drink. Helmut's eyes were even greener in his room, and he fixed them on her. She'd seen that look before. In Moro's eyes, in Adnan's eyes. Could he really be interested in her? Shaibu had kept hinting at it, but she'd brushed it off as Shaibu's eternal silliness. She'd never trusted Helmut and his people. Wurche refused the next round of drinks. She needed to stay clearheaded.

"What are your people doing here?" she asked, the drink pushing the words out of her, erasing the politeness she'd been trying to maintain.

"Wurche, not now," started Shaibu.

Wurche said when she was young they never saw people like Helmut. Yes, there were people with pale skin, but they were just like her people—same kind of hair, just stripped of brown color. Then suddenly it seemed as if, day after day, more pale people with unusual straight hair and multicolored eyes were showing up. "We were told that you would protect us. But from what?"

"From people like the Asante," said Helmut, his face red. "The Asante dominated you for decades ... Your own father told me this."

"We can fight our own wars," said Wurche. "And you say you are helping us, but how are we to know it's not to take over our land and drive us away?"

"If we wanted that, we'd have fought a war," Helmut said.

"Enough," said Shaibu.

Helmut grabbed a roll of paper from his table, sat by Wurche and spread the sheet in the space between them. It was a map. The inscriptions were not in Arabic, like the maps Jaji had shown her. This one was bigger and showed places she hadn't seen before, some shaped like chicken wings.

"This is the whole world," said Helmut. Various places had been marked in ink: in the western and southern parts of Africa and parts that lived in the blue of the ocean. He pointed to Europe, then slid his finger down the curvy dome of Africa, and said if he'd traveled that distance in a ship, it had to be for a good reason.

"My people moved, too," said Wurche. "And it was to conquer other people."

"It's about friendship," said Helmut.

Wurche wasn't convinced, but she was tired. When Helmut offered to walk her home, she didn't refuse, and at her door, he pressed his lips to the back of her hand. She wondered if he would be more honest if Shaibu were not around. So the next day, she asked Aminah to prepare tuo with baobab powder soup, a dish Helmut relished. She put the bowl of tuo and jugs of millet beer in a basket, clasped the basket's handle over her arm, and took zesty strides to the barracks.

"Good day," she greeted.

"Good day," the first guard said, his almost transparent eyes slitting with suspicion. She wondered if he was the one who had allegedly spurned Hafisa, the woman who sold boiled groundnuts wrapped in outdated Gold Coast newspapers. Hafisa had given birth to a child the color of one of her own nuts, and when she'd gone to the barracks after pushing the baby out, the guard would not even look at her. Wurche asked for Helmut, but he was not there. As she handed the guard the basket, a chilly gust of wind suddenly swooped down. The sky darkened and trees that had seemed sturdy swung from left to right. Wurche ran, pellets of water splashing her cheeks. By the time she got to her door, the rain was pouring in sheets and had soaked her. The weather in Kete-Krachi was often like that: violent and unpredictable. She peeled off her wet clothes and slunk into bed, waves of dejection washing over her. Her mission had failed. Her thoughts drifted to Kpembe, as they always did when she was alone and often after a difficult day. When she'd first arrived in Kete-Krachi, Mma had sent a messenger begging Wurche to return. There was no message from her father, her husband or her brothers. It was comforting knowing that one person still cared for her, but a word from Etuto would have carried more weight—she wanted to know that her father missed her, needed her. And yet, nine months had gone by and not a peep.

Later, Wurche took the flimsy manuscript of a Nana Asma'u poem to bed in the dim light of the room, with the sound of the river lapping in the evening's quiet. She always read through the poems first to get a sense of their themes before copying them for Jaji—even though they were ultimately always about a person she was not: a good woman. She preferred doing her own reading, about people such as Alexander the Great, but Jaji's library only held fragments of such literature. She'd barely started the first line when claps cut through the silence. She went to the door and met Helmut's beaming grin. In his hand, a small lantern. He thanked her for the tuo and asked to take a walk with her. She changed into a smock and riding boots.

The smell of ash, dawadawa trees and rain lingered in the air. The sky was pitch black—the moon nowhere in sight—but spangled with stars. They said nothing to each other as they edged towards the river. She wanted to ask him again what he was doing in Kete-Krachi, but not with the combative approach she'd used before. She had to learn to be patient.

"You don't mind if this is a long walk?" said Helmut.

"I wore my riding boots."

A herd of cattle grazed on the bank, their long horns like a garden of thorns.

"The Fulani believe that cattle come from water," she said. "They say a water spirit impregnated a woman who lived by the river. In those days, cattle lived in water. The spirit drove the cattle from the water for his human children. He taught them how to herd the cattle and breed them. That's why you always see Fulani people with cows."

Helmut asked if Aminah was Fulani. Wurche, who had never asked Aminah where she'd come from, said, "Yes, from somewhere around there."

She was embarrassed that she knew nothing about the person who took care of her child. About the person whose beauty was invading her dreams. Was Helmut, too, in love with her?

"She works very hard," he said.

Wurche wondered where the conversation was going. The walk needed to end if he'd invited her to ask about wooing Aminah.

"Why did you say that?" she asked.

He hesitated, then said, "I read a dossier with information on the region, in which the Fulani were reputed to be lazy. The report said they would rather lord it over others and own slaves, mostly because they were some of the first converts to Islam."

"And it said what about Gonjas?"

"Only that the name came from the Hausa word for kola."

"There's more."

"And perhaps yours being a higher civilization because you're Muslims. One group was described as having a despot for a king and his people, drunkards."

A hint of triumph passed over Wurche, quickly replaced by annoyance. What was this big dossier? And why lump a whole people as lazy or hardworking or drunkards? She knew people in Kpembe who worked the land till their joints grew stiff and she knew people who drank till their lips turned pink.

They reached a part of the river where felled logs lay. Wurche lowered herself onto a log. The rough ridges of it poked her skin. Helmut sat too, placed the lantern on the grass and inched towards her. She wanted to push him away. She wasn't in control of her insides. Her emotions were spilling out, all over the place.

"Do you have the dossier?"

He shook his head. "I read it in Germany."

It would be good to know what kind of white people were coming to places like Kete-Krachi, and if they were there to help or if it was for their own benefit. She had to stay calm.

If she got angry, she would upset him and lose the only link into their world. She asked him about his family.

His father taught in a place called a university, a school for adults. His mother raised his five siblings and him. He thought his parents lived uninteresting lives, so after completing the year of required army training, he volunteered to stay on, which is why he got sent to Kete-Krachi. He grew up in a town called München, also by a river, like Kete-Krachi. He was recently made lieutenant, but still felt like he mostly took instructions.

"Nothing exhilarating," concluded Helmut. "Now tell me, how does a princess from Salaga end up in her enemy's camp?"

"Running away from a husband she was forced to marry. What else has Shaibu told you?"

"He says good things about you. That you used to beat him in horse races when you were younger."

"Is he doing anything about my horse? Are you? It's been over nine months."

"I haven't heard anything about a stolen horse yet. We get a lot of cases of livestock. Sheep, cows."

"Some time ago, there was a man caught for stealing a cow. Aminah told me you referred the case to the imams. Why didn't you just arrest him?"

"Because your imams are to you what priests are to us. They are important for keeping the peace, and we don't want that to change."

"And the Dente wasn't important for keeping the peace? You executed one of our religious leaders. To me, it seems like you are pushing us against each other."

"It happened before I came here, but I heard he was anything but peaceful."

Wurche stretched her arms to the skies. The European strategy was definitely divisive. She observed Helmut. He seemed an honest man.

Later, he walked her to her door, and again pressed his lips to her hand.

Outside Jaji's house, two dogs sniffed at each other. One was small and black, the other big, with a mottled brown coat. The big dog tried to mount the small dog, but the small dog wasn't having it and barked. The big dog backed off, went off to a tree, lifted his hind leg and let out a stream of urine. The small dog chased after the big dog and started sniffing him again, tried jumping on him. The big dog, encouraged, tried again to mount the small dog. The small dog snarled. And on the dance went. Every time they drew close to Jaji, she flapped her straw hat at them. Wurche saw a white dog approach from the distance. The small dog ran up to it.

"That little dog is flitting from one dog to the next," said Wurche. "A true flirt."

"There are too many of them," said Jaji, fanning herself with the hat. "Apparently since the Dente was executed dogs now run this town."

"How so?"

"Remember for a long time he didn't allow in many outsiders. It's the traders who brought in the dogs."

It made Wurche think of Baki. She brushed off the thought because she didn't want her good mood ruined. Jaji relished Saturday mornings, when she didn't have to teach Koranic school or the women of Kete-Krachi. And Wurche liked her teacher best on those days, when she could sit by the learned woman while keeping stock of her business. Sales were so good that they had invested in more chickens and Wurche was able to pay Aminah a small cut. Small, because she had to save. Aminah collected the chickens' eggs into baskets and sold them raw, boiled, and fried. Women bought the raw eggs, children on their way to Koranic school liked the boiled eggs, and men loved the fried eggs inserted into canoes of bread (and spying on Aminah, Wurche imagined).

The dogs yapped at each other. As she watched them, she asked Jaji why she hadn't remarried after her husband died. "You surely have urges," said Wurche.

"When you find me locked up in my room, I'm surmounting those urges. Besides, I'm not sure a husband will understand the work I do."

"Aren't you lonely?"

"I don't have time to be lonely," said Jaji. Wurche didn't believe her. Jaji didn't even have close companions. Her extended family lived near Sokoto, a two-week journey away. Even though Jaji, Shaibu and Helmut provided company, it was nothing like what family brought. Wurche missed her father and brothers and Mma. She was glad she had Aminah, her quiet companion, whom she now saw approaching from the market, holding Wumpini's hand, a basket hanging from the elbow of her other arm. She handed over the cowries from the sales she'd made and headed into the house. Wurche wondered what went on in the girl's head. She had never seen a frown pleat Aminah's face. She wore a quiet smile that wasn't always happy, but was pleasant and grounded all in her company.

"Stop it," said Jaji, startling Wurche.

Wumpini had grabbed a stone and aimed it at the dogs.

"Don't be cruel," said Wurche.

"They'll bite me," said Wumpini. Her chest ached. She didn't want her son to be a fearful person. If Mma were around she would say it was because Wumpini was growing up without the authority of a father. When she was younger, she wondered if growing up without a mother had made her hard, as the women of Kpembe often described her. Now, she didn't believe any of it, because she'd had a mother: Mma had taken care of her. If anything, what Wumpini was missing was the closeness of family, where everyone played a role in raising a child. The sooner they returned to Kpembe, the better. She had to work harder to get information out of Helmut, to understand what the white men wanted, and she had to make more money.

Wurche decided to personally deliver a basket of eggs to the barracks, hoping to find Helmut. Usually Aminah did the delivery. She gave the basket to Bonsu the cook, an Asante man who had lived in Salaga before the war broke out.

"It's not a good day," said Bonsu, seated before a big bowl of dishes flecked with food. His cheeks were wet with tears.

"What's wrong?"

"The Asantehene has been captured and the English are exiling him to some Seychelles place."

Wurche hadn't always been sympathetic to the Asante because they had demanded so much of the Gonja, but rather them than the Europeans. Now the Europeans had defeated the most powerful king in the region; who knew what they could do next? The door whined open and out came a pasty soldier, followed by Helmut, clutching his empty breakfast plate. She patted Bonsu's back and waved at Helmut. His face reddened and he waved back. She asked if they could take a walk that evening. He nodded and went back inside. The interaction had been strange. Helmut had been more guarded than usual.

Perhaps because his fellow white man was around. When Bonsu thrust Wurche's basket in her direction, his eyes were like small ponds. He shook his head and went back to scrubbing dishes.

That night, Wurche was determined to keep the mood light, to extract as much out of Helmut as possible. She even answered his prying questions about her marriage, which he likened to that of a European queen called Catherine the Great. Helmut said, almost conspiratorially, "After she ran away from her husband, she took on a lover."

Wurche froze. Had Moro rejected her and then gone on to blabber about their affair? She didn't really care if Helmut knew. But if Helmut knew, surely Shaibu did, too, which also meant all of her father's enemies. And that she didn't want. If Moro had told Shaibu, she *would* turn into a murderer like the so-called Catherine the Great was rumored to be. In broad daylight, she would use the musket Dramani had given her. But when Helmut took her hand, she understood what he meant. *He* would be the lover. Wurche suddenly felt stupid.

Helmut said, "I was pleased you asked me to go for a walk. I've been trying to find a way to spend time with you. Alone. But I wasn't sure if it was the right thing to do ... Or if you were interested."

He swallowed the last word. He had turned the color of a fish's gills.

"There are too many constraints," said Wurche, thinking out loud. What she didn't add were the words, *even if I were really interested.* When he looked perplexed, she held up her hand against his, pointed to the skin enfolding them. "This. What would happen if we had a child?"

"We don't—" began Helmut.

"It wouldn't end well. Look at Hafisa." Wurche thought of the poor woman, who was looking more wretched by the day, with her yellow-skinned child. The image sparked her. "Your guard spurned her. You and your people can do whatever you want. It doesn't matter to you whether I'm the daughter of a chief or the daughter of a commoner. You can do what you want because you have powerful guns and even more powerful people protecting you. You say you're here to bring us friendship and protection, but I've seen the way your people—English or German—talk to our chiefs. There is no respect. The Asante king has been exiled. For what? Defending his land and his people? You told me you are here for friendship, but that is not the way to treat a friend. Can you tell me the truth? Why are you here? And why are you competing? English, French, German. Why don't you leave us to handle our own affairs?"

Helmut looked at his feet, his face purple with embarrassment. Time stilled. The silence between them was like the air on a humid day. Cloying.

"I'm sorry," said Wurche, ashamed about her outburst. "You have been nothing but kind to me and Jaji. You have shown us friendship and been open and wonderful. I am simply trying to understand what's happening to us. If you would look at things from our point of view, you would see that we are being forced into new ways of living and it's confusing."

"I understand," said Helmut. "I promise to be as honest as I can with you. The way I see things, we benefit from you as much as you from us. It's an exchange."

"An exchange, I could handle. But what bothers me is you telling us how to live. I'll give you an example. Before your people arrived, slaves were people caught in war or people whose families couldn't take care of them. A lot of them married into even royal families. After you came, it became a business. Kidnapping, raiding. Those things were started to meet your needs. Now, all we hear is how you Europeans want slavery to end. In other words, you're calling *us* the bad ones."

"You may be right," said Helmut, "about the hypocrisy."

He admitted that many became prosperous from slavery and even the abolition of it. But he believed the good outweighed the bad. "We are working on building schools in Kete-Krachi and making sure that children stay in school," said Helmut. "In Lomé, we've built railroads, we've built roads and bridges. If you ever make it down there, you'll see what Kete-Krachi could look like in a few years."

Wurche looked into his eyes and saw he was earnest. He believed what he was saying. And yet, she wasn't sure the other white men, like those who had exiled the Asantehene, shared Helmut's belief. He held her gaze. The sound of water slapping the riverbank crept into the quiet that was again growing between them.

Then Helmut did the strangest thing. He palmed her cheek and pressed his lips to hers. It wasn't the way she and Moro had expressed their feelings for each other—they'd pressed their foreheads together. Fleetingly, it troubled her that he had so easily moved on from the conversation—it made him seem insincere. But she liked how she felt.

When she caved in to his advances, it was out of curiosity, out of defiance, out of hoping it would get her back home. It happened again and again.

*

"I need your advice," said Wurche.

Jaji peeled her gaze away from her manuscript. The teacher didn't like to be interrupted when she was reading, but now was the time to ask. Aminah wasn't there and neither was Wumpini, who had started repeating everything he heard. Jaji nodded for Wurche to go on.

"Is it bad that I have Aminah?"

"How so?"

"Is it wrong for me to have a slave?"

Jaji lowered her manuscript onto her lap. She pressed her fingers under her chin and hunched her shoulders.

"There's a story I very much like about a philosopher and an old man. The philosopher says to the old man, 'I have a bird in my hand; is it dead or alive?' The old man responds, 'The life of the bird is in your hands.'"

Then Jaji picked up her manuscript. Why couldn't the woman just say yes or no? Wurche supposed that it meant that Aminah's life was in her hands. Was that a bad thing or a good thing? Helmut was telling her it was bad. From that riddle of a response, she supposed, Jaji agreed with Helmut.

Aminah

Aminah had just bought Wumpini a colorful beaded necklace at the market and yet he pointed to a small drum with black rope crisscrossing its body, next to a collection of koras and flutes. Aminah tut-tutted and grabbed his hand as he reached for it. He always wanted things, a small disappointment for Aminah, who suspected that this greed came straight from Adnan. Only greed could have made Adnan as fat as he was. The minor disappointment came from the fact that she'd come to regard Wumpini as family—he was as good as a son to her, the only family she had. Like any mother, she wanted the best for him and at the same time, projected her hopes and dreams on to him. Despite her disappointment, she indulged him when she could afford it.

It was as loud and crowded as any market day. They walked past mats of rusty guns, axes, rolls of cotton and tie-dyed cloth, sandals, cones of shea butter, glass, baskets, balls of tobacco of the kind Eeyah had used to get to stuff her pipe. Soon, they arrived at the livestock market.

"Asalaam alaikum," she greeted the butcher, who was chopping slabs of meat. He nodded at her. "Mutton, goat head, cut into pieces like you always do, and cow foot."

She began negotiating, a dance she both enjoyed and detested. It pleased her to get a good bargain, but she didn't like the long process it involved. She looked about for Wumpini and, when she didn't see him, she stared wide-eyed at the butcher, who simply shrugged. There was no knowing what Wurche would do to her, and she didn't want to find out. She scanned the scene before her: a barber holding a blade close to a Mossi trader's skull; green water streaming down the market soil; a mangy brown dog lapping from the stream; a woman with dried fish spread on her cloth; a man selling metal tools. And there, Moro, holding Wumpini's hand. Her heart climbed back from her stomach.

Outside Jaji's, she often ran into Moro. Usually, he appeared seriously involved in something, so she or Wumpini noticed him first. She didn't want to encourage the thought that something larger was pitting their paths in collision. That whole business of licabili. He'd look up and smile, and when that happened she'd scurry away, not in fright, but because of her conflicted emotions. Her attraction to him. The repulsion she felt for who he was. The fact that she had to forgive him. She thought of Eeyah on the floor of their compound, of Issa, of the twins, of Na and the baby roasting to death. She was not yet ready.

"Wumpini!" She rushed to grab his hand, nodded a hasty greeting, and went back to the butcher.

"It's my fault," said Moro, suddenly at her side. "I waved at him and he ran to me. Give my sister the best parts, o!"

The butcher snorted at Moro, slapped the goat head on his board, and hacked it to pieces. Aminah studied the morsels of meat, the flies that wove around the butcher, the large sheep's carcass hanging in the back of the stall, against the braided grass wall. Anything to not have to speak to Moro. When the butcher handed Aminah her meat, she placed it in her basket, smiled to indicate she was on her way, then dragged Wumpini in the direction of the barber. She looked back. Moro had already disappeared into the throng of market-goers. She exhaled.

Because he hadn't pressed her for anything, Aminah panicked less when she saw Moro after that encounter at the butcher's. She let him accompany her for short distances, but only if she had Wumpini by her side. She hadn't decided how she wanted him to fit into her life. Soon, she found that Moro was generous and Wumpini benefited greatly from this arrangement. Moro bought him the drum he wanted. Next, an ostrich feather. Moro always bought kola to give to the blind beggars in the market.

One evening, after delivering eggs to the barracks, she saw Helmut seated on the veranda with a fellow white man smoking a pipe similar to Eeyah's. Before she could stop him Wumpini was on the veranda. Helmut picked him up and tickled him and he responded in giggles. Aminah froze. She would have approached had Helmut been alone, but the other man, with his thick mustache, seemed gruff. And whenever she went to the barracks, the guards hurried her through the back, where Bonsu the cook worked. She'd never been on the veranda. The gruff man burst out laughing. Helmut waved at her to come over. She curtsied and pried Wumpini from Helmut's grasp.

"Sister will be waiting for us," she said.

Helmut stood up and tickled Wumpini's belly, rippling laughter through the boy again.

"Off you go, then." He walked down the steps of the veranda, then touched Aminah's arm. "Perhaps, it's not my place to say this, but I will say it anyway: Moro really cares for you." His eyes searched hers for a reaction, but she didn't know what to say to him or what to do with that information. She already knew it, but to hear it confirmed was at once comforting and frightening. She needed a friend. She needed to have her feelings chewed and digested by another person before she could make sense of them. In Botu, when she had continually mentioned Motaaba's name, her friends let her know she liked him. But it was a short-lived infatuation that ended when she began menstruating. Suddenly, Motaaba appeared too immature, with his crocodile-hide disguises and skinny legs. This time, she would have told her friends that the problem was that men like Moro had broken up her family, had broken her. It seemed foolish to love a person like that. What was the line between forgiveness and foolishness?

Meanwhile, the emancipation they'd heard about from the Gold Coast wasn't spilling over the river into Kete-Krachi. People still sold slaves in the markets, captured people were still in boats on the river, and Wurche had said nothing about setting Aminah free. Jaji had told Aminah to wait, but it was making her impatient. Waiting made Wurche annoying: the way she swallowed water, letting a little gulp escape from her throat; the way she spoke, rounding out her mouth and dotting the corners with her thumb and forefinger, made Aminah want to lash out and scratch her. And just as soon as she had those thoughts, shame would flood her. On days like that, it was best to stay away from Wurche. Aminah would walk to the market, Wumpini's tiny hand clasped in hers, her other hand clutching the precious cowries she had earned from selling eggs.

Wurche wasn't giving her a lot—which could have been another source of Aminah's irritation—but she decided to start saving. Birds built their nests little by little, and so too would she. Maybe, she could buy her freedom without having to wait for emancipation to arrive in Kete-Krachi. She would be so proud to be able to do that.

The smell of a chicken coop: eggy, meaty, fecal; an unusual combination of foul and pleasant. A million clucks and squawks. A coop full of droppings. Aminah wondered why she was strangely attracted and repulsed by the smell of the place. It wasn't downright putrid like the excreta of other animals—the pigs of Wofa Sarpong, for instance. Still, after more than five minutes in the space, she had to hold her breath. And all that noise! Chickens were talkative.

"A nice surprise," she heard. Wurche's voice. Aminah couldn't leave the coop for fear that Wurche would think she was being nosy. She was forced to keep inhaling the coop's odor. She heard Helmut mumble a greeting.

"You've never come here this early," continued Wurche. "It's nice to see you in morning light."

"Yes," said Helmut, his voice unusually stiff. "Listen. I just heard this and wanted you to know, because you have every right to know. And because I care about you. And I promised to be honest with you."

"What is it?"

"A group left for Salaga early this morning. Your father has apparently breached the agreement he made with us. He accepted the British flag some years ago, and when one of our generals recently tried to extend ours to him, he refused. I don't know what they are going to do in Salaga, but they were heavily armed. I am going up to Dagbon with another group. We have been given orders to make sure the paramount chief accepts our flag with whatever means we need to use."

Aminah felt like she had smeared chicken feces in her nostrils. There was no longer anything pleasant about it. She took back her initial opinion.

"I have to go back," said Wurche.

"There's nothing you can do. You're safer here."

"I have to warn them."

"They'll be in Salaga faster than you can get there."

A feather flew straight into Aminah's nostrils. She sneezed violently.

"Aminah," Wurche snapped.

Aminah opened the door of the coop and walked out. Helmut was in a green uniform and cap, with a gun slung over his right shoulder.

"I can't stay. Please don't do anything rash."

Then he reached forward and pressed his lips to Wurche's. She stood there with her hands at her sides, looking like she'd been forced to eat a teaspoon of fermented dawadawa. And yet, it was a moment so intimate, so private, Aminah was forced to look away. It explained Wurche's absences.

"Don't repeat this to Jaji," said Wurche when Helmut left. Aminah waited to be lambasted for eavesdropping, but Wurche said nothing more.

Later that evening, Wurche paced the length of the small courtyard. She hadn't touched her dinner. Jaji greedily swallowed huge morsels of tuo. The learned teacher did not possess one cooking bone and so was very happy when invited to join Aminah and Wurche's meals.

"How do I get back?" said Wurche.

"Are you sure you should be heading there so soon?" asked Jaji. "Not everyone will be as kind to you as Shaibu. Your father has many enemies and if the Germans are in Salaga, they have definitely gone with some of Etuto's enemies who know you."

"If the Germans have already attacked, I'm sure Etuto's enemies wouldn't be looking for me."

Aminah saw a door opening. By the time Wurche returned from Kpembe, she could be long gone. If the Germans attacked Salaga, Wurche and her father—if he was still alive—would be too weakened to worry about a runaway. The problem was Wumpini. What would happen to him? Jaji could not take care of him.

"I'll go to the stables tomorrow to get transportation for us," said Wurche, ending Aminah's scheming. "We should leave by the end of the day. Aminah, pack all our bags."

"It's too risky," said Jaji. "Wait till you hear news. Or at least pack only some of your things, in case you have to return."

"We'll have Wumpini with us," said Wurche. "People are nice to mothers with children."

Aminah wanted to give Wurche a lesson on people. The horsemen hadn't cared about mothers or children. But her having said that made Wurche seem softer, more receptive. Aminah had never seen her so subdued.

"What if you go and it's wiped out?" asked Jaji. "Will you come back? Why don't you wait for news?"

"I have to go back. They haven't always been good to me, but they are still my family."

Wurche went back to her hut.

Aminah followed. "Sister." Wurche regarded her. "I want to stay in Kete-Krachi."

"So do I," said Wurche. It wasn't the response Aminah had been expecting. She thought she would be told that she was needed to care for Wumpini. Instead, Wurche added, "I thought I would make something of myself before going back ... I need you in Kpembe."

She hadn't said the right thing. She should have said she wanted to be free.

Aminah stuffed her belongings and Wumpini's in a cloth sack. Next, she tied up the chickens, as Wurche had instructed, and put them in two baskets. Everything was happening so fast, and it filled her with panic and sadness, made her angry with herself for not being bold. It drove her in search of Moro. Maybe it was also seeing Wurche and Helmut in that intimate moment. It made her ready to forgive Moro.

She went to Shaibu's. He lived in a cluster of huts as palatial as Etuto's abode in Kpembe. The Germans had built it for the new Salagawura, and Shaibu and Moro also lived there. Shaibu's face remained as cool as a rock when Aminah told him the Germans were going to attack Salaga. She was acting reckless, she was sure, but it didn't seem to matter. It was as if the world were ending and there was no time to waste.

"Where's Moro?" she said.

"The market."

She combed through every corner of the market, looking at every tall figure that came by. She found him studying a hoe by the metalware seller. She tapped his shoulder and when he turned to regard her, she blurted out, "We're going back to Kpembe."

She told him about the Germans going up to Salaga and that Wurche wanted to waste no time in getting there. But she would rather stay in Kete-Krachi. She wanted choice. She wanted freedom.

"What would you do if you were me?" said Aminah.

"I have been in your situation," said Moro. "In many ways, I still am. I grew up in one of the slave villages of Salaga and Kpembe, in a place called Sisipe. So I am considered a descendant of slaves. I was very young when I was taken to live in the Kpembewura's palace. My parents thought I was lucky to be taken under the former king's wing. They didn't even protest when I told them he had recruited me to raid villages when I came of age. My father said everybody comes onto the earth to fulfil a number of tasks. Life will lead you to that place, so do each task well and let life take care of the rest."

Moro paid for the hoe he'd been looking at. The seller wore round wires over his eyes, a piece of jewelry Aminah had never seen before. What about the two of us, Aminah wanted to ask him. Why had their lives been linked if she was going to be sent far away? She was finally letting that thought bloom: that their paths were linked for a reason.

"In Salaga," she said, "why didn't you take me then and why didn't you come back?"

"I saw you and thought you were beautiful. And that it was sad that you were with that short, ugly man. I didn't know what your relationship was, at first. When I found out he was about to sell you, I made an arrangement to buy you. I didn't have enough money because Shaibu had asked me to buy him smocks in the market from the sales I made. I couldn't go back to Kete-Krachi without the smocks. My plan was to get my pay from Shaibu and return in three days with the money to finalize my exchange with Maigida, but Shaibu didn't pay me for a week, and Wurche had already bought you by the time I got back to Salaga. It seems like Shaibu's my friend, but I'm really his servant. Royals never let me forget that I am descended from slaves.

"When I returned to Salaga, I was angry with Maigida, but thankful he hadn't sold you to a stranger. Then I heard that Wurche had moved to Kete-Krachi. I had to find out if she'd brought you with her. I was the one who begged Shaibu to go to Jaji's to pay our respects and there you were, even more

striking than when I first saw you. It seemed like destiny was
working in our favor."

"And now, it's pushing me away again," Aminah said, despite
herself. "So I get to Kpembe and then what? I won't stay a
slave forever. Unlike you, I wasn't born into a life of servitude."
Aminah regretted her words. She'd meant no harm.

"I am going to Sisipe," he said, "to farm the land. When
you told me I shouldn't sell people ... I heard you. I had been
trying to get out for a while, but your words were the push I
needed. Go to Kpembe because she needs your help. Then
ask for your freedom. Keep asking. She'll hear you too. After
that, you're welcome to come to Sisipe if you'd like."

He reached out, timidly at first, then firmly pressed Aminah's
shoulder and let it go.

That afternoon, Wurche, Aminah and Wumpini sat on a
cart laden with their belongings and chickens and headed for
Salaga. Aminah hadn't realized that Wurche wasn't the wealthy
woman she'd first met. She was surprised that they couldn't
even afford their own donkey. It was sobering and made her
feel sorry for Wurche, made Aminah glad she was still with
her for the return to Kpembe. When Wurche and Wumpini
had settled back into life in Kpembe, if it was still standing,
Aminah would ask to be set free.

The donkey cart came to a stop in front of a building that the
cart owner claimed was the Lampour mosque. It was pocked
with bullet holes like a starlit night, and the owner refused to
go on. Wurche argued with the man and tried to get him to
take them to Kpembe, but he said it was his last stop.

"It smells like burnt tuo," said Wumpini, as Aminah took him
down from the cart. At nearly four, he was taller and trimmer,

but still carried his weight in his bones. She retrieved the two baskets of chickens and looked about. Wumpini was right. The air reeked of ash. It reminded her of the day she'd lost her home. A few steps ahead, she made out a naked corpse. The cart almost ran over it as it departed. Aminah held Wumpini close and pressed her palm over his eyes. In the distance, gunshots sounded. *Ka-ka-ka-ka*!

Wurche rooted through one of the sacks and brought out a long gun. She thrust it into Aminah's hands and told her to wait while she arranged for them to get to Kpembe. Aminah looked at the gun, inscribed with Arabic. It was a weighty object she could have done without. It didn't make her feel any safer.

"Why is everything broken?" asked Wumpini. "Where's Mama?"

"Some bad people came to burn the place," said Aminah. "Sister will be back soon." Everywhere they turned was a stack of broken-down walls and thatch and cinders. It would be a miracle if Wurche found transportation. Aminah put the gun down, but immediately picked it up when a man covered in soot approached them. Where was Wurche? But the man kept walking.

Wurche strode over with someone Aminah thought she recognized. They got closer and Aminah wasn't sure what to say to him. He was, after all, the person who had brokered her sale.

"Maigida," she said coolly.

"You look well," he said, then turned to Wurche, who pointed at the chickens.

"Maigida has kindly agreed to keep our chickens until I can come back for them," explained Wurche. "We have to walk to Kpembe."

Aminah placed the chicken baskets in Maigida's back room. While the rest of Salaga had fallen apart, it was a room conserved in time. It was whole and had kept its moldy fermented smell. How many lives had been exchanged in there? Where were they now?

They left Maigida's and began the trek to Kpembe. On the narrow streets of Salaga, people bent over piles of smoking rubble, their clothes torn and filthy, and gathered the charred remains of their lives. One man lowered a pot into a well and rinsed the soot off his face.

"Another well!" exclaimed Wumpini.

"Salaga is the town of one hundred wells," said Wurche.

"Why are there so many wells here?" asked Aminah.

"They were built to wash slaves after long journeys," said Wurche.

A town created to sell human beings, thought Aminah. A town like that could not prosper. It was probably why Salaga had suffered so many wars.

"What are slaves?" asked Wumpini.

I am your mother's slave, Aminah wanted to say.

"People who are owned by other people."

"Why ..."

"Wumpini, save your energy," said Wurche. "We have a long walk home."

What should have taken just under an hour became a two-hour long punishment. The road was blocked with stones piled high, and twice, white men in the same uniform Helmut wore had set up their caravans. They were laughing, some of them even half undressed and cooking. They didn't look menacing, but Wurche took out her gun and herded Aminah and Wumpini into the bush at the side of the road.

They crossed the forest where Aminah had learned to mount Baki and where Wumpini had practiced his walking. Patches of black and brown had replaced the beautiful green that had once covered the forest's floor. Trees that had once seemed grand were now dry, charred at the roots.

By the time they reached Kpembe, Wumpini was covered in dust, Aminah had a splitting headache, and Wurche was walking faster than ever, steps ahead of Aminah and Wumpini. Aminah would have the done the same if she were in Wurche's shoes. At the palace, the main halls were intact, but the huts in the outer ring had burned down. Even the two stones that used to guard the entrance had disappeared. Cautiously, gun held out in front of her, Wurche led them into the inner court. Mma was folded over the well close to Sulemana's room, one hand on her back, the other reaching for the a pot in the well.

"Mma," said Wurche, lowering the gun to her side. The old lady whipped herself around, then clasped her mouth, dropping the pot into a thousand shards. She came closer and her eyes filled with tears.

"Oh, thank Allah! Alhamdulillah. I expected the worst."

"I expected the worst, too," said Wurche, embracing her grandmother.

Mma struggled to pick up Wumpini, squeezing him in a tight hug. She leaned over and hugged Aminah. Then she turned to the compound. "Maraba, maraba, maraba! They've come back!"

This eventually drew out Sulemana and some of Etuto's younger children. Etuto was the last person to come out of his hut. Aminah marveled at how, in two years, the tall man had developed a stoop, his shoulders hunched as if invisible hands were pushing him down. His skin was sallow and blotchy. And he had shed the weight that once made him appear frightening. All in the compound watched with bated breath. Etuto wrapped his arms around Wurche. Aminah was surprised when a loud sob issued from Wurche. She was glad no one had been hurt. She was happy for Wurche. It also meant that Wurche didn't need her. She could ask for freedom.

Wurche

Wurche hid the soft swell of her belly under large smocks. She had been vomiting for a few weeks. At first, she thought it could be explained by nerves. Then she thought she was adjusting to Kpembe's well water. A few weeks later, in her mirror, she saw a round bump sitting unusually low on her belly. She did everything to avoid Mma's scrutiny, and the only thing that worked was foisting Wumpini on the old lady.

She was glad to be back with family, especially since Adnan had returned to Dagbon. With glee, Sulemana recounted how her husband had demanded his bride-price be returned, refusing to go back to Dagbon empty-handed. A wife with royal blood or his bride-price. He stayed in Wurche's room for close to a month and was only placated when Etuto used his powers as Kpembewura to force a lesser chief to give up a daughter to Adnan. In retaliation, that chief defected to Kete-Krachi, as had many of Etuto's once-trusted soldiers. That and the German attack had proved costly to her father, a fact Wurche was sensitive to since she hadn't helped her father's health by running away. She was now determined to stay and do everything in her being to appease him.

But the baby embedded in her womb was not going to help.

Only Aminah had noticed Wurche was carrying. The girl feigned ignorance for a while, then asked one evening what

Wurche was going to do when the baby came out. Wurche pretended she didn't know what Aminah was talking about. Of course, the baby would cause a stir once she delivered it, the way everyone knew, from the light, iroko-wood skin of the Kete-Krachi groundnut seller's baby, that the father was a white man. But that was no reason to get rid of it. Helmut had been good to her, shown her tenderness in a way neither Adnan nor Moro had. She had kept convincing herself that she was sleeping with him to learn German secrets and tactics, and a minor infatuation didn't hurt—it propelled her—but she was also sad to be away from him, from his gentleness and honesty. But soon it was clear their dalliance was never given a chance to develop weight or complexity, because her sadness faded when she saw her family: Mma with Wumpini; Etuto, in spite of his frailty; Sulemana. Aminah.

One morning, terrible contractions made it impossible to keep the secret in her belly hidden any longer. Wurche barked at Aminah to fetch Mma. Pain tore through her body and she held in a scream, settled on the floor, and exposed her belly. She thought childbirth got easier after the first time. When Mma arrived she clasped her mouth, then gathered herself and sent Aminah to get the midwife and her assistants from the house across the street.

The baby was small with a full head of curly hair, and at first, no one remarked on her color, since most babies came out looking pale.

But by the first week, the baby's skin hadn't baked into a deep brown; if anything it had grown lighter, the hue of shea butter kissed a golden brown by the sun. And the baby's eyes were clear like glass, with flecks of green. After eight days, when

Etuto was allowed to see the baby, he came in and wordlessly walked out of Wurche's hut.

"They are talking about me, aren't they?" asked Wurche. Aminah was wiping the baby as Wurche rested in bed. She looked at Wurche and opened her eyes wide. "I have a white baby and they think I'm a whore."

"Sister, people say your baby is beautiful."

"And my father? He hasn't given a name. He hasn't said a word to me." Wurche paused. Milk issued from her breasts and stained her cotton blouse. She fixed her eyes on the orange whorls stamped on the door's curtain. The snail-like shape repeated in almost translucent patterns even as she shifted her gaze to Aminah. "Can you believe that I didn't know who Wumpini's father was at first?" She paused, read Aminah, who shifted her attention from the sandy brown baby on the bed to regard Wurche. "If it was Adnan or if it was Moro."

Aminah stiffened, then went back to wiping the baby. She lifted the little girl's fat thighs and swiped her buttocks.

"But soon it became clear Adnan was very much his father."

Relief washed over Wurche. The intention was not to hurt Aminah, but to fulfill her own selfish need to tell somebody who knew all parties involved. Also, there was something about confessing to Aminah in particular that provided catharsis. She wanted Aminah to hold her. To just hold her. Instead, Aminah swaddled the baby in linen and handed her back to Wurche.

"You're not upset I've told you this, are you?"

Aminah shook her head.

"You never say anything. Tell me how you honestly feel."

Aminah paused.

"I've already forgiven Moro," she said, finally. "And I don't think you're a whore. You've loved several people and that's not a crime. I saw the way the baby's father looked at you. It reminded me of my parents. He loved you ..."

Then Aminah frowned and wrinkled her nose.

"What is it?"

"I want my freedom."

Aminah left the room before Wurche could respond.

Two weeks went by and Wurche's baby still hadn't been named. At first Wurche thought Etuto was going through one of his bad moments, but when she saw his messenger coming out of his hut laughing heartily, she stormed in.

She greeted him, curtsying with all the politeness she could muster.

"Wurche," said Etuto, regarding her from where he sat on his pouf. He didn't get up to embrace her or smile or point to some new gadget he'd been gifted. His eyes were puffy and red. The vapor of alcohol hit her where she stood, more than an arm's length away.

"Etuto, my baby has no name."

"The father names the baby." He whisked a fly off his cheek.

"The baby's father is not here, so the grandfather takes on that role."

Etuto studied Wurche for a long time.

"Name it what you like," he said.

Wurche's heart ached. Her father had never been so cold to her.

"Please," started Wurche.

"What do you want me to say? First, you take off, making me look like a fool before everyone from here to Dagbon. It was fine when it was other people defecting, but my own blood? Let me finish talking. I understood, eventually. Your spirit and Adnan's spirits were not matched, and I was forcing you to kill your spirit. I got over that betrayal. But this I don't understand. These people have destroyed me. Us."

"I have no explanation. But, I need your blessing. Do it for the baby."

Wurche got on her knees to beg, but Etuto stood up, grimacing as he straightened his back. Life was funny. She, who had mistrusted the white man, now had a baby whose father was white. Her father, who went to the white man with open arms, refused to accept one of their children.

"Well, as they say, the child of a whore will be a whore too."

He went into his inner room. Wurche watched the curtain settle back into place and swallowed the gulp that had blocked her throat. All her life, she'd been afraid of this one unsaid fact of her mother's identity. It didn't bother her as much as she'd expected, but it angered her that her father thought he could use it to insult her.

Days later, she decided to name the child Bayaba, after her mother.

Since Bayaba's birth, silence had wrapped around the compound and tightened its downy grip, especially on Wurche, who was considering going back to Kete-Krachi or somewhere on the Gold Coast, near the sea. She'd heard that women with children like hers were not a rarity there. Etuto had sent Sulemana there to meet the Gold Coast governor and Wurche had wanted to go with him, but Mma begged her to hold on until the child could walk.

Wurche wanted to tell Aminah that she had set her free, but she would wait until Sulemana returned. She needed to have at least one person on her side.

Because it had grown so quiet in the palace, the wail that shook the compound awake a few days later was so loud, so deep, it rang in the ears even after it had stopped. Wurche threw on a smock, left Bayaba sleeping, and went outside, where a messenger was kneeling before Etuto and Mma. Etuto, as still as a pot of water, was staring above the messenger's head, not even a ripple shaking his body. The wail had issued from Mma. Aminah was there, holding Wumpini's hand.

"What's going on?" asked Wurche.

"Something has happened to Sulemana, but it was said in Gonja, so I didn't understand."

"Sulemana and the others have been killed," Mma said in the same tone Jaji's students used when learning their lines. "At Yeji. We don't know if it was bandits or your father's enemies."

"It's not true," said Wurche. "It can't be ..."

"I'm finished," said Etuto. "This is the end. They are coming for me."

Her legs grew weak, as if a sharpened spear had stabbed and twisted her spine. She held on to Aminah and then couldn't take any of it any more. She turned towards her room. Finally, she understood her father's disease. It was when the world lost all color, taste and smell, and one realized the heaviness of one's body, the uselessness of one's life. Wurche stared and stared at the wall. Would she be dead, too, if she'd gone with them? Would her presence have warded off death? The questions swirled. Sulemana was never coming back.

She wove in and out of sleep filled with woolly dreams. The only sharp detail that day was the single gunshot that cut through the air. Close, and yet distant. Final, and insistent on its finality. One could think of nothing but the crispness of the sound. Outside, just enough light traced the sky for her to make out the forms of huts and trees and people, but otherwise, it was dark. People flocked outside Etuto's hut. Had they come about Sulemana?

"Excuse me." She was making her way through them when Aminah blocked her.

"Sister, please. It's not good."

"If you've seen it, so can I." Wurche pushed forward but Aminah wouldn't budge. "Let me by," she said, her voice breaking, as if she already knew. She shoved Aminah so hard the girl fell.

The scene: blood; a mother and her child; a mother and her son. Mma had wrapped her arms around Etuto's body. The offending rifle lay, indifferent, on a leopard skin. Wurche hugged Mma and Etuto's lifeless form.

His heart had been broken, she decided.

Etuto and Sulemana's funerals were attended by people from all over Gonja and Dagbon, and even several white men from the Gold Coast. Dramani came back from the farm and, as the man of the house, greeted the invited guests and accepted their condolences. The funeral was a blur. It was only after the bodies had been wrapped in cotton shrouds and buried that Wurche realized what was happening. Power had shifted in Salaga-Kpembe and Kete-Krachi. All over.

"There's a vacuum here," said Wurche to Mma, who had never seemed so childlike as in that moment. The old lady had responded to visitors with whimpers and barely spoke. Wurche went on. "The infighting among our people, this struggle between us and the Europeans. It's all about finding power, exercising power, holding on to it at all costs. The Europeans are a force bigger than our tiny lines. The only way we will mean anything is if we unite. I've been preaching unity for a long time, but I haven't tried to work with anyone. I'm ready to start talking to the women of Salaga. We'll rebuild together. Tell the elders. They'll listen to you. Enough people have died. It's time to work together."

Mma nodded.

Aminah

She went to the well by Sulemana's room, dipped a round clay pot into the water and filled it to the brim. She grabbed a broom and approached Etuto's hut. No one in the family had been able to face the task of cleaning his room. Even though she'd never considered Etuto a father figure, it felt like she was coming full circle, doing what she couldn't do for Baba and his workroom. Immense, whereas Baba's was small, but plain whereas Baba's was etched with beautiful black-and-white lines. She parted the heavy curtain and went into the room. After Etuto shot himself, women from Kpembe had taken the body and wiped away the gore, but the metallic odor of blood lingered. It was even stronger than the leathery smell wafting from Etuto's hides and shoes. Guns were slung all over the outer room, and Aminah pictured the knives on her father's wall. One was a den of creation, the other of destruction. But ultimately, both men were no more. Both men had left behind everything they owned. Whatever you did, whether good or bad, death would eventually snatch your spirit away. So what did you do when given a choice? Good or bad? Eeyah used to tell her that if she chose to be bad, her spirit could come back in a very ugly body.

She shook out the thick, musty cloths that covered Etuto's bed and folded them. She wiped down his many riding boots, some of which had become nests for geckos. She arranged his empty bottles of alcohol in a corner. She left his piles of talismans and charms, too scared to touch them. They were said to render him invisible.

When she left the hut, she was filled with such a sense of loss that she had to go into her room to cry. She cried till her eyes felt rubbed raw, till she couldn't breathe, her chest pushing out hard to let in air.

Two weeks later, Aminah cleaned Bayaba and handed her back to her mother. Mma had taken Wumpini under her wing as if that would replace Etuto.

"Aminah, you're free," said Wurche. "I should have told you this a long time ago, but with the funerals ..."

Aminah saw, for the first time, that Wurche must have liked her, possibly in the way she had liked her sisters, quite possibly in the way men and women liked each other. She reached forward and embraced Wurche, whose matchstick body only stiffened more. Wurche patted Aminah's back. It was enough, the gesture said.

"Thank you, Sister," said Aminah.

"Take one of the hens," said Wurche.

"Thank you. Can I come back and see Wumpini?"

"Yes." Then a beat later, "Where will you go?"

"To Moro."

Aminah cleaned out her room and put her things in a sack— clothes inherited from Wurche, money she had saved from selling eggs. When everyone was sleeping, she took the hen and left the palace. She didn't want everyone staring at her as her back grew smaller and smaller.

She walked the path to Salaga, and once there, went past the big mosque, towards Maigida's hut. She stopped to contemplate what would have happened if someone else had bought her. If it had been Moro or if she hadn't met him at all. Where would she be? Her life had been treated as if she were no different from cattle or kola nuts. Stripped of control.

She continued past more huts, the two markets, now dead except for scavenging dogs. The Germans had killed the town. Even in her short stay in Salaga, she'd been intrigued by how much was sold there. Her heart felt weighed down but then, almost a heartbeat later, light. This was a new start. She started dreaming of a shoe workroom, one that she and Moro would build, that she would decorate to remind herself of Botu. She would make shoes to sell, while Moro worked the earth, and their children would grow up learning to create and live with the land. And then, one day, her father would come by on his albino donkey and say he lost his way home.

Gratitude

To my family for always saying yes, no matter how far-flung my dreams. Abdul-Rahman Harruna Attah, Nana Yaa Agyeman, Rahma Harruna Attah, Pierre Alexandre Poncelet and Emile Saha, you rock. To the Gee and to the Hot Gyals, thank you for your friendship and support.

To the Pontas Literary and Film Agency family for constantly pushing hard for me. Anna Soler-Pont, Marina Penalva, Maria Cardona, Leticia Vila-Sanjuan, and Jessica Craig: thank you.

To my publishers, Judith Gurewich and the wonderful Other Press team, and Cassava Republic, thank you for believing in my project.

To my first readers: Jakki Kerubo, Mohammed Naseehu Ali, Anissa Bazari, Ayi Kwei Armah, and Max Lyon Ross.

To Pierre, for the beautiful map. Mille mercis.

To the Africa Centre and Instituto Sacatar for the time you afforded me to write and for the magic of Bahia. To Natalia Kanem for beautiful KSMT, for the magic of Popenguine.

And, finally, to my late Uncle Muntawakilu, my guide to Salaga. My gratitude knows no bounds.

Q & A for *The Hundred Wells of Salaga*

1. **What inspired you to write *The Hundred Wells of Salaga*?**

Some years ago, I learned that my great-great-grandmother had been enslaved and ended up in the Salaga slave market. Attempts to find out more about her led to obstacles. People either simply didn't know much about her or they didn't want to talk. Writing this book was a chance for her to finally speak through me. I calculated that she might have lived in Salaga during a turbulent period in the region's history. Not only were different families—known as gates—competing to rule over the area, but Europeans also wanted access to Salaga as their link to the interior of West Africa.

2. **We know so very little about internal slavery in Africa compared to the transatlantic slave trade. How did you carry out your research for the novel? Did you have to visit an archive in Salaga itself?**

I first visited Salaga in 2012. A late uncle of mine guided me through its slave market, now turned into a lorry station; to its ponds where slaves were washed before they were sent to be auctioned off in the market; to the hundred wells that dot its landscape, now watering holes for livestock; and to its museum, which houses some of the chains that held people captive as well as the guns used in capturing them. Most of the sites were covered with weeds. The museum was run-down. It was obvious not many people knew about this aspect of history that took place in Ghana.

I did a lot of reading, spending several days at the Schomburg Center in Harlem and the Balme Library in the University of Ghana. Some useful guides were J. A. Braimah and J. R. Goody's *Salaga: The Struggle for Power*, Braimah's *The Two Isanwurfo's*, and Marion Johnson's *The Salaga Papers*, which was a treasure trove of accounts spanning decades of Salaga's history, written by missionaries from the Gold Coast and European travelers.

This novel focuses on a period right before the war in Salaga in 1892 until the downfall of Salaga to German forces in 1897. It was a dramatic era because not only were different families vying for the throne of Salaga, but also because the Europeans (British, French, and Germans) were making their way into the zone, following the Berlin Conference of 1884–1885. The area had initially been declared a neutral zone, but European powers breached their own agreement and started signing treaties with the local chiefs.

Through my research, I learned a lot about internal slavery in Africa. By the time in which this book is set, slavery—both internal and transatlantic—had been legally abolished; however, as the book shows, it was still a thriving business. People like Samory Toure and Babatu became infamous figures because they refused to succumb to colonial forces, but were also fiercely tied to the institution of slavery. The royals in *The Hundred Wells of Salaga*, much like Toure and Babatu, benefited from the drawn-out struggle to abolish slavery. In the Gold Coast, for instance, slave-owning families wanted reparations from the British government for losing their slaves.

3. This book is as much about the internal feud among royalty as it is about slavery, and it gives us an insight into a certain African courtly society. Why did you think this was so important to write about?

I wanted to write about this because we haven't dealt with how a lot of African royal families were complicit in the slave trade. I read accounts that give us a free pass, because "African slavery was benign." The reasoning behind this thinking is that, unlike in places such as the Americas, a slave's child would usually not become a slave. However, in indigenous slavery in Ghana, slaves *were* given names that to this day paint them with a mark. Other justifications for such thinking include the fact that a slave could marry into a family, which made it different from the slavery across the ocean. But families *were* torn apart. Peoples' lives were discarded if they were not deemed profitable enough.

Bondage is bondage and I want us to talk about the past and deal with it. Not dealing with this past means it rears its ugly head every so often. In 2017, when the world heard that people from countries such as Senegal, the Gambia and Nigeria were being auctioned off in Libya for as little as $400, it seemed from another era; one that had been buried, hopefully never to be unearthed. And yet, slavery was still alive and festering. Everyone was outraged, as they should be. But in addition to outrage for me was shame; according to an April 2017 report led by the UN International Organization for Migration (IOM), these auctions were facilitated by people from Ghana and Nigeria. I wanted to bury my head in shame. But it meant it is time for us to wake up. We have to acknowledge the role we've played in slavery—internal, trans-Saharan, transatlantic— and how that has fostered a distrust that persists in our communities to this day. Only then can we begin to stitch together the threads we need to heal and achieve true progress.

4.   The book is from the point of view of Aminah and Wurche, two very different characters who occupy vastly different social positions in the book. Yet you provide a very complex and interesting relationship between the two. What were you trying to achieve when you were writing their relationship?

History has written about women like Wurche. We know about Queen Aminah of Zazzau, of Queen Nzinga of Angola, of Yaa Asantewa of the Asante, and even earlier, Queen Tiye and Hatshepsut in Egypt. The feats of royals have been written down on stone or immortalized in song and passed on by griots, and because of that, I had material to work with for writing Wurche's life. There were precedents. Aminah's story, on the other hand, I had to search for within myself. European explorers barely gave women any space in their written works, so nonroyal women's stories were hard to find. Even though the royal story has always seemed glamorous, on digging a little deeper, one realizes that women still had a bad deal. For one, we can readily count the number of queens or women warriors the continent has seen. I wanted to highlight that even though they were from different worlds, being a woman meant that they still suffered from similar fates. Aminah comes to this realization and is able to be more forgiving towards Wurche. Wurche, on the other hand, never admits this to herself. The two women grow close, maybe because of this, but it's a relationship that lives in what is not said; the two women are often quiet around each other. Wurche's shyness is a complex blend of feeling superior to and being attracted to Aminah, while Aminah's combines a strong yearning for her freedom with compassion for her captor.

5. **If you had to choose between the two women, who would you rather be friends with, Aminah or Wurche?**

I would probably gravitate towards Wurche just because she's so confident and does what she pleases, and that is attractive. But if I needed a confidante or a kind ear, I'd go to Aminah. So I can't choose!

6. Jaji is Wurche's teacher, but she is also an intriguing character. Can you say more about your motivation for including her character and was she inspired by any historical figure?

I love mentors. Having benefited from mentorship almost my whole life, I see Jaji's character as a nod to the amazing women, and men, who've guided me through life so far. And yes, jajis actually existed. In the late nineteenth century, Nana Asma'u was the daughter of Usman dan Fodio, who founded the Sokoto Caliphate in northern Nigeria. She trained a group of female teachers who went from village to village teaching women Muslim values and urging them to be good mothers and wives. The jaji often went on to train other teachers. She wore a unique straw hat, so that she could be identified, and used poetry to teach these values.

7. In literature, imperialists are often villainized, and portrayed as greedy and without regard for the lives of the conquered people. In Salaga, the German character Helmut was presented as a complex and sympathetic figure. Was his character based on a real-life person? What were you trying to do with such a multifaceted portrayal?

Helmut is a hundred percent fictional. One of the critiques I received from earlier work was how flat some of my male characters came off, so with this book, my goal was to create fully rounded people. I also didn't want to have outright villains, because even the kindest people are capable of cruelty, and people tagged as evil can do the kindest acts. I wanted a character who was flawed, but who could at least question himself and the way his fellow countrymen were behaving.